MARIE-HÉLÈNE LEBEAULT

AUTHOR OF THE EVERS SERIES

THE QUEST

— FOR THE —

SACRED TREE

DEFENDERS OF THE REALM - BOOK TWO

BEACHES AND TRAILS
PUBLISHING

ABOUT THE AUTHOR

Marie-Helene Lebeault lives in Quebec, Canada and is the mother of two young adults. A retired teacher, she now spends her days writing, translating academic manuals, and lending her voice to corporate training videos. She enjoys reading, hiking, and going to the beach. She is also an avid rollercoaster fiend and is on a mission to visit all the Six Flags amusement parks with her daughter. Every year, she travels for three weeks on a solo adventure to a new part of the world.

Follow on Social Media, she'd love to hear from you!

Website Email Newsletter

facebook.com/mhlebeaultauthor

x.com/mhlebeault

instagram.com/mhlebeault

amazon.com/author/mhlebeault

bookbub.com/authors/marie-helene-lebeault

goodreads.com/mhlebeault

linkedin.com/in/mhlebeault

tiktok.com/@mhlebeaultauthor

youtube.com/@mhlebeault

ALSO BY MARIE-HÉLÈNE LEBEAULT

The Chronicles of the Starborne Cadets

Stars Beyond Realms

Shadows of Orion

Echoes of the Void

The Nebula's Heart

The Starborne Paradox

Defenders of the Realm

A Journey to Power

The Quest for the Emerald Rattleback

A Summer of Discovery

The Quest for the Sacred Tree

A Summer of Opposites

The Quest for the Phantom Feather

A Summer of Courage

The Quest for the Kraken's Ink

A Summer of Destiny

The Quest for the Cursed Mirrors

The Evers Series

The Ancestors' Key

The Academy

The Time Walker

The World Jumper

Blood Magick Trilogy

The Blood Mage

Blood Magick

Blood Legacy

Standalones

Clarity Castle

What Happens Next?

Ghost Stories

Holiday Shifters

Echoes of Tomorrow

Utopia

Picture Books

Fairy Grandmother: Millie Goes to Antarctica

Fairy Grandmother: Millie Goes to the North Pole

Fairy Grandmother: Millie Goes to China

Fairy Grandmother: Millie Goes to Africa

(Also available in French, Spanish, German, and Italian)

CHAPTER
ONE

KAIA BOLTED UPRIGHT IN BED. She screamed as she lifted her hands to ward off the invisible attacker. She could almost feel the sharp edge of the sword slice through her skin, tearing muscle from bone.

Then the glow of the light stone on her nightstand flared brighter, illuminating her bedroom. No attacker. No shadowy figure of the Odentian captain who had hunted her and her fellow student-witches through the Silent Marshes last year. She was home. She was safe and sound, and nobody wanted to harm her.

Sweat drenched her nightgown as her pounding heart slowly went back to normal. She took deep breaths, calming herself as her hands continued to shake.

"It was just a nightmare," Kaia told herself. "Just a nightmare."

It had felt so vivid, though. She shuddered as the images came back to her. Finnegan, his plumed helmet outlined by a blazing fire, as he lifted his sword above his head. It had been almost a full year since the attack, yet Kaia's nightmares hadn't ceased.

She was almost afraid to lower her feet off the side of her bed, as though Finnegan might be lurking in the shadows beneath her bed, like a monster from her childhood fears.

Footsteps sounded outside her door. Images of the Odentia captain flooded her mind; he crept up to her door and tried the handle.

Kaia screamed again, a blood-curdling tear against her throat as the handle turned—only for it to be cut short when the door flew open, and her father rushed in. His silver eyes swept over the room as he made his way to the bedside.

"It's all right," he said as he sat on the edge of her bed. "It was just a dream."

Tears burned Kaia's eyes. She threw her arms around her father and buried her face into his shoulder. She had thought that the best part of him being home all summer would be the fun adventures they could get up to... she never expected that she would end up clinging to him like a child at least once a month.

What am I going to do when I get back to the Institute? I'll end up waking up the others every night!

Papa stroked her silvery curls, murmuring comforting words. Despite his reassurances, Kaia could still hear the lingering worry in his voice. It was all too stark a reminder of the conversations she'd overheard between him and Mama, wondering if it was wise to even send her back to the Institute.

As comforting as his presence was, Kaia couldn't help but feel frustrated with herself at the same time. She kept a journal of her fears, talked to a therapist, did her breathing exercises, and filled her mind with positives before going to sleep.

So why wouldn't these nightmares stop?

It was embarrassing to be reduced to tears over dreams that she knew weren't real at fifteen years old. By this point in her life, she had thought she'd already learned how to handle her fears on her own.

Finnegan had been sent back to Odentia. He wasn't even in Eldavon anymore, and there was no reason for him to sneak into the schloss just to find her, anyway. It was ridiculous; she knew she was safe... but she didn't feel safe. She hadn't for quite a while now.

Kaia wiped her eyes and pulled away from Papa, forcing herself to smile. "I'm sorry for waking you up."

"I was already awake," Papa replied, tucking a strand of hair behind her ear. "Would you like me to sit with you for a while?"

She did, but that was beside the point. The darkness outside and the bags under his eyes told her he was exhausted, and she didn't want him to think she needed to be babied any more than he already had. Even though he never made her feel childish, she knew it was.

"I think I'll just read for a while," she said, forcing herself to remain bright. "Go on to bed, Papa. I'll be fine."

"If you're sure?"

Kaia nodded her head firmly. She would make herself be sure. Papa kissed her forehead and left the room again, closing the door softly behind him. As soon as he was gone, Kaia pulled her knees into her chest and searched the room again, looking for anything that might be out of place.

All was in order, as she knew it would be.

"I want to go back to school," she told herself aloud. But even to her own ears, it sounded as though she was lying.

It wasn't entirely a lie. Kaia did want to return to the Institute and see her friends and learn more magic. But at the same time, she didn't want to leave the safety of the schloss, her parents, and her tutors. What if more bad things happened this year, like they had the last two?

Whenever she visited the Institute for her cousins' graduation ceremonies, she always felt safe there. But she had always felt safe, regardless of where she was. Now it seemed like the world was far more unpredictable than she ever realized, and Kaia was uncertain how to face it.

Dread was her constant companion these days. Perhaps, once she was at the Institute and her mind was full of magic and learning, it would get better. That was the best she could hope for, at least.

Kaia laid back down and reached for her book. She didn't open it, though, unable to even think about reading. Right now, she knew reading wouldn't be enough to banish her nightmare. But what would? She didn't want to write about it in her journal, either.

She turned over, staring at the far wall as she tried to think instead about what the year at the Institute would be like. Normally, she had no trouble thinking about everything she was looking forward to. But the dim light muted her thoughts. Kaia sank back into an uneasy sleep.

BABY REUEL WAS ONLY one month old and still had what Penelope's sister, Julie, called the 'newborn scrunch.'

Penelope smiled at the sleeping baby in her arms as she rocked in the chair Julie's mate had made for her. She couldn't help but feel a sense of peace and calmness in these moments. The house was quiet, and she had her precious little nephew in her arms. He was heavy for how tiny he looked, his wrinkled little hands tucked up close to his face.

He was also like a tiny furnace. But Penelope found she didn't mind so much. It was a cool, rainy day outside, and she was fine with the extra warmth that Reuel provided.

Normally, Penelope wasn't left looking after the baby, even though she enjoyed helping to take care of him. Today, though, everyone else was busy with the Fire Watch, and Julie needed some time to herself. As a dragon, her body was healing nicely after giving birth, though Julie was still recovering. She didn't have much time to just go out for a walk or nap.

Penelope was only too happy to give her older sister the opportunity to rebalance herself. Julie's emotions were all over the place these days, making Penelope feel bad for her.

"And you're easy to look after when you're sleeping," Penelope whispered to Reuel. He scrunched his nose as though he was about to wake up, but Penelope rocked him, and he settled down again. It was amazing to her how relaxed a baby could be.

He was just about the only person who was relaxed here at home.

The tension was becoming unbearable. Ever since Penelope had told her family that she intended to join the military instead of the Fire Watch as all of them had, there had been an undeniable current of anxiety in all her interactions. It didn't help that she had told them all on the same day that Julie had planned to announce her pregnancy. Though Penelope had had no way of knowing that, Julie had yelled at her about it.

Since then, they didn't really talk about it much. But every time Penelope brought up training or the Institute, there was a clear sparking tension in the air, the sort that made her terrified another fight would break out. It was like catching the first sniff of smoke on the wind.

Penelope sighed, adjusting her hold on Reuel to hold him a little closer. Her determination to join the military had only increased since he had been born, though Julie had point-blank asked her how she could think about military service when she clearly loved her nephew so much.

"I don't know how to tell them it's *because* I love you so much that I know I have to join," Penelope whispered, her brow puckering.

She knew that as the youngest child of her parents, she had a different perspective than they did. She had also gone through more than they had... first, being kidnapped by Odentian warriors in the heart of Eldavon near the sacred Silver Springs. Then, the first-year witches being attacked and hunted last year in the Silent Marshes...

Why couldn't they understand she felt the need to protect the Kingdom?

"Can't they understand how much it hurts when I overhear them talking at night, listing all the things they can do to change my mind?" Penelope grumbled.

The comforting warmth of the baby wasn't so comforting anymore. She was worried her increased tension would interfere with Reuel's sleep, so Penelope carefully stood and tiptoed to his cradle, where she laid him down. He looked so cute in his little sleeping sack.

Penelope crept from the room. Julie and her mate, being new parents, had been given a cabin that the Fire Watch used rather than the tents. The rain pattered on the wooden roof as Penelope carefully ensured the door was open an inch so she could hear if Reuel fussed.

Then she started to pace down the hallway and back up, wanting to release some of this restless energy that had crept into her.

The thing was, she had always had a very clear expectation of her future. From when Penelope was young, she had copied Julie and Benton in talking about how she would join the Fire Watch. She had never expected, never wanted, a different path... even now, she didn't want to join the military so much as she felt it would be her best choice.

She only wished her family could understand how difficult it was and support her rather than argue with her about it... it made her feel extremely alone in carving out this path.

Penelope ended up feeling like it would be a breath of relief to be away from her family, which was an unsettling sensation. Yes, she looked forward to being with her friends and learning at the Institute, but she hated that one reason she was looking forward to the school year starting was so she wouldn't be around her family for a while.

It just didn't seem right.

The front door opened, and Penelope turned to see Julie step in, shaking out her long hair. Julie's eyes had dark smudges underneath, but her cheeks were rosy, unlike the pallor that had been in them when she left.

"Was the baby good for you?" Julie asked, her tone stiff as she took off her coat.

"He slept the whole time," Penelope replied. "He's still sleeping, actually. I can stick around if you want to nap. I know you haven't been sleeping well."

Julie gave her a wan smile. "Thanks. He should wake up in about half an hour to eat... if he doesn't, you can let him sleep. The doctors say he's at a healthy weight and advised me to sleep when I can."

Penelope nodded. "Go nap, then. I'll get some supper started for you."

"Thank you, Pen." Julie stumbled toward her bedroom. She paused at the door and looked back like she was about to add something.

Penelope tensed. Would Julie say something about the military again? But her sister only shook her head and stepped into her room. Penelope let out a heavy breath as she took a moment to release her tight muscles.

Soon, she thought. *I'll be back at the Institute, and I won't have to worry about this anymore.*

CHAPTER

TWO

EVEN THOUGH THE medical wing at the Institute had received no patients today, Wickham still went through the same cleaning procedures to end his shift. First, boil water and add in the antiseptics. Then put on a fresh pair of leather gloves, which also had been boiled in antiseptics but were now dry, and start scrubbing down the work surfaces.

He hummed as he worked, enjoying the routine. Even the smell had become pleasant since he had learned that he could add eucalyptus without damaging the cleanser's effectiveness.

He'd been here at the Institute for two weeks now, even though classes wouldn't start for just under a month. Every day, students were trickling in. Wickham would have been one of the last people to arrive; only he had gotten a part-time job here and needed to start before the semester got going so he'd have time to adjust.

It was certainly a novel experience to voluntarily be away from his family. Over the last couple of years, he'd argued and fought for a way to study from home. But he knew it was the right choice to be here now, and he was proud of himself.

While he never thought of himself as 'dependent' since his focus was always on helping his family, Wickham certainly felt like it was growth to look beyond his individual circumstances. The village herbalist, Kassandra, had little more she could teach him as she wasn't a true doctor, and Wickham was determined to enter the medical field. Though he often thought of his time in her little shop. She had been a valuable mentor.

It was the best way he knew of how to serve the Kingdom... and he'd be able to take care of his family better that way, too.

The door to the medical wing opened, and his friend, Herja, sauntered in. Her short black hair was slicked back and shone in the light from the light stones arranged in the ceiling. She wore a black tunic and trousers with her usual bookbag slung over her shoulder. Today, she was wearing an obsidian fox pendant on a leather chord.

"You going to be much longer?" she asked as she settled into one of the waiting chairs.

"Not long," Wickham replied.

His heart thudded as he appreciated the look of Herja's black ensemble. She had confessed to him she chose all dark colors like this to avoid having to figure out what colors went well together, but it looked good on her. It reminded Wickham of the powerful aura of the dragon king, Lantos, when he addressed the students.

He would never dare say it out loud, though. Herja didn't like it when he complimented her.

Wickham shook his head and went back to work, ignoring the heat in his cheeks as he dipped his cloth back into the hot water. The fluttering in his stomach he'd got when he thought of Herja over the summer was only getting worse now that they were in close contact with one another again. She was so smart, so brave... and beautiful.

Trying to put that from his mind, he overly scrubbed one counter. Cleanliness was paramount for the well-being of the patients, after all.

It was a difficult adjustment, but he'd settled into his role here and was determined to fulfill his responsibilities seriously. It was a rare opportunity for a second-year student like him to get a job in the medical bay, and he was determined to prove himself capable and deserving of the position.

The rustle of the pages of a book caught his attention, and he turned, finding Herja reading.

Her nose scrunched up the way it did when she was really concentrating on something. From where he was, Wickham couldn't tell what she was reading. But he admired the way her lips moved silently as she read, the way her eyes darted across the page with intensity. It made him want to watch her forever—

She looked up suddenly, and Wickham jumped, his face growing hot as their eyes met. Herja frowned at him.

"What is it?" she demanded.

No way was he going to admit that he was staring because he found he enjoyed looking at her. That was a recipe for disaster. If Herja didn't like him complimenting her, she certainly wouldn't enjoy hearing that confession.

"Is there something on my face?" Herja asked, wiping at her mouth.

"Uh... yeah," Wickham said quickly, latching onto the suggestion. And a good thing, too.

Herja wasn't interested in him that way, and he valued her friendship too much to mess it up because he couldn't stop staring. No, he would not think that way at all. Besides, at the end of the school year, they would go through the mating ceremony that would show them who their perfect matches were.

Wickham wasn't going to let himself build up false expectations only to be disappointed. His mate deserved better than that.

What if I'm matched with Herja?

He pushed that thought aside as he turned back to his work. "Actually, I just remembered that I have extra chores I have to get done. I'm going to be another hour at least."

Herja groaned. "But I'm so bored! I was hoping we could play a game."

"Sorry," he said over his shoulder, focusing intently on his scrubbing, though he had already cleaned the spot thoroughly.

Herja huffed as she put her book back into her bag. "Fine. I guess I'll see you when you're done."

She left again, and Wickham leaned against the counter, letting himself heave out a deep breath. As much as he thought he would make a good match with Herja, it wasn't up to them to decide who they were matched with. He could make a good match with the other dragons, too.

The stars would decide who his fated mate was. And until he knew who that was, he would not let himself feel any of these emotions. It wouldn't be long now, and then they'd know. He'd know... and then he could figure out what happens next once he knew.

IT HAD BEEN WELL over an hour, and Wickham hadn't shown up to the dorm. When she swung back to the medical wing, she found he wasn't there, either.

Herja was put out with her friend, but Wickham kept busy. He'd probably show up later with a good reason for his disappearance. In the meantime, she went out to one of the picnic tables, making sure she was alone before she pulled out her secret notebook from her book bag.

Normally, this wasn't something Herja would hide from anyone... but over the summer, she had devoured several novels that, while they had adventure in them, were primarily romances, she had to admit.

Now she was trying to write her own. She already had the characters. The heroine was a plucky orphan, much like herself, who was chosen by the ancient gods to save the Kingdom from the evil king, who would end up being her father. And then there was the hero, a pirate with a heart of gold who stole from the hordes of the rich to give to the starving poor...

Herja groaned as she rested her head in her arms. The heat of the sun beat on the back of her neck. She fell asleep each night thinking of the dramatic scenes between her two characters. But every time she opened her notebook, her thoughts simply stopped.

And what little she had written, she desperately wanted to share... but was far too embarrassed to actually let anyone else read it.

Lifting her head, Herja picked up her pencil. What she really wanted to do was skip to the scene where her heroine and hero kissed for the first time, but that wasn't until the end of the book, and she was barely at the beginning. She couldn't just skip all the in-between stuff, could she?

"Ugh," she growled at herself. "As though I have time to waste on all this sloppy romance nonsense, anyway!"

She snapped the book shut and tossed it back into her book bag. Herja pulled out one of her textbooks, along with the notebook she was using for this class. This was a much better idea, she decided. Writing would not help her proceed in life...

And besides, she was only interested in writing romances because she was so deathly terrified of the mating ceremony at the end of the year.

After only half an hour, she reread the same page what seemed like a hundred times; Herja reluctantly closed her textbook. It appeared she would not be able to distract herself at all.

"Shucks, geeze, golly-whiz!" she said aloud, thumping her fist on the table.

A stern voice spoke behind her. "Excuse me? What are you using that language for?"

Herja turned to find Professor Farrow, the first-year dragon teacher, approaching. Their eyes were narrowed seriously, but Herja had gotten to know Row well enough to see the teasing lines at the corners of their mouth.

"Just wait," she said, scowling fiercely. "I'm about ready to say things like *crappy*."

Row snickered as they slid onto the bench across from Herja. "I take it you're feeling rather frustrated with something?"

Herja sighed. Sometimes it felt childish to use these terms, but she didn't like swearing... even if sometimes she felt like it would express herself better. *Doesn't really matter, does it? I don't enjoy using that language.*

Row tilted their head to one side. "Are you mentally avoiding the topic?"

"Yes."

"I see.... So does that mean you don't want to talk about it?"

Herja shook her head, but it wasn't because she didn't want to talk about it. Rather, it was because she didn't want to want to talk about it... and she was confusing herself with all her thoughts.

"I'm afraid of the mating ceremony," she finally blurted. "I don't want to do it. I don't want any of it... I'm better off on my own; I always have been."

Row folded their hands on the picnic table. "Are you, though? I thought you enjoyed having your friends."

"I got to choose who my friends are, though," she muttered.

Row nodded with a gentle smile. "I understand. It's been a long time since I went through the mating ceremony, but I was a nervous wreck that whole year. I looked at all the witches in my year and tried to imagine what my world would be like if they were my perfect match. Everyone offered something different."

"I talked to Headmasters Twila and Valiant," Herja said slowly. "They told me about their final year here at the Institute and how they ended up getting along... they told me that regardless of who I'm matched with, I need to let the relationship develop naturally and not put too much emphasis on the potential romance."

Row nodded again. "That's good advice. My mate and I didn't start dating until a few years after we graduated. In fact, I almost married someone else."

Herja frowned. "No, you didn't."

"I did!" Row laughed. "Fifteen is a little young to fully understand how complicated love can be. Not that you should fight it. But letting your relationships develop naturally is the best course of action."

"You know that doesn't actually help me, right?" Herja asked, tracing a pattern on the tabletop. "I don't know how to do that, and all the books I read are useless. It's always either at first sight, they're instantly in love, or suddenly after they nearly die, they realize they're in love."

"That's because books aren't real life, Herja."

Herja scowled at them. Of course she knew that!

Row gave her another gentle smile. "I know it's not helpful; unfortunately, all I have to say is that the stars already know who your perfect match is. You can't force it; all you can do is prepare by improving yourself."

Herja sighed. Row was right. It was hard for them to be helpful when Herja wasn't entirely certain where her fears originated. Best not to think about it at all... she had a lot of work to do this semester, after all.

THREE

KAIA HID a yawn behind her hand, hoping that nobody would notice how obvious her tiredness was. She had arrived at the Institute late last night and had been so worried about waking up her roommates that she barely slept.

"Are you okay?" Wickham asked next to her.

Kaia gave him a smile. "I'm fine, Wick. I was just so excited to start the school year," she lied. No use in burdening him with her problems. She straightened her shoulders as their professor strode into the room.

Kaia was a little disappointed that they had a different professor every year. She had gotten along well with Professor Lee last year. But each year, they had to learn new skills, so it was better for a new teacher who specialized in those skills.

"Greetings, second-year witches!" the professor boomed as he came to the front of the room. "Let's see... I believe we have all met."

He adjusted his glasses and pointed to Kaia. "Kaia, Wickham, Icarus, Adina, Lena, and Jalene. Only six students this year. It was an off year for babies, it seems. This last summer, we have over a hundred children make the trip to the Silver Springs; we have nearly twenty dragons and witches each."

Kaia's brow furrowed. She knew their year was unusually small but didn't expect it to be the topic of conversation on their first day.

Professor Avery adjusted his glasses again, the lenses flashing with light. "Well then. We all know that we'll be going to the Golden Forest this semester, yes? I'll be teaching you how to harvest raw wood with magic so as not to harm the tree. Then, you will each find a Pheonix Gingko to harvest from; you will make your own pages for your spell books to go with the Emerald Rattleback skins you harvested last year."

Last year. Kaia couldn't help but flinch. It was a fluke that she and Wickham had come across a Rattleback shedding its skin and could collect it for the entire class.

Thinking about that, Kaia couldn't help but nervously glance at her classmates. Icarus had been injured, nearly killed, protecting her from Finnegan. He didn't seem to still be suffering, but how could she tell how bad his scar was beneath his shirt?

"We will study word-based spells while at the Golden Forest," Professor Avery continued. "After the winter break, we will spend the rest of the school year in the classroom honing those skills."

"And then at the end of the year is our mating ceremony, right?" Adina burst out. She straightened in her seat, her intense gaze locked on Professor Avery.

He chuckled in response. "Yes. But I would advise you not to think about that too much. Focus on your studies."

But what if Finnegan came after them again? What if Odentia sent more warriors to attack them? Kaia pressed her palms together. Her fingers were freezing cold, but her clothes still grew damp with sweat.

"How can we focus on our studies when your futures will be revealed, you may ask," Professor Avery said. He strode back and forth in front of them, his booming voice filling the room. It drove Kaia's thoughts from her head; when the professor spoke, she had no choice but to listen. "It's simple, dear students. I will not tolerate sloppy work. You had good old Lee last year, and he's a delightful chap, but I believe in rigorous work. If I feel you're behind where you should be, I will assign extra classes to you. If you value your free time, you will not slack off."

Kaia raised her hand.

Professor Avery turned to her. "Yes, Kaia?"

"The second-year dragons—our future mates—are going with us to the Golden Forest, correct?"

"Indeed, they are."

Kaia frowned. "So, if we're living and studying in close quarters with the people who will, in less than a year, be revealed as our fated mates, how are we supposed to focus? My mother says that fifteen is the year that hormones really start kicking in... and that they can't be controlled through sheer force of will."

Professor Avery looked a little surprised for a moment, or maybe he was just trying to school his expression. Kaia squinted. Was he fighting laughter?

"Why do you think I'm so tough on my students?" Professor Avery asked with a wink. "Don't worry. You'll soon be too stressed out about your marks to worry about mates and all that. And I can assure you, the dragons will feel the same."

Herja and Penelope, of course, would be there, just as they had been the previous year at the Silent Marshes. Then, there were Odele and Nolen, the twins. Finally, Xena and Vera.

Who could be her perfect match? She was already friends with Penelope and Herja. They got along well, even if she sometimes got annoyed with Herja's tendency to talk over everyone else. She sort of knew Xena, or at least knew she had been named after a famous warrior-queen of days gone by, and was determined to live up to that name. Vera mostly kept to herself. Odele was very much like Herja; only she seemed a little more intuitive with other people's emotions. And Nolen... Nolen was nice, but Kaia couldn't remember anything specific about him.

She brought her mind back to Professor Avery as he continued. "My mate, Professor Sabelle, will work them just as hard. And you will all need to be vigilant with the Chameleon Sprites."

The Chameleon Sprites. Mama and Papa both liked to tell stories from their second year when they went to the Golden Forest and met the Chameleon Sprites. Apparently, they were rather mischievous but fun to be around.

When Kaia glanced at her fellow students, though, she was surprised at the apprehension on Wickham, Adina, Icarus, and Lena's faces. Jalene looked eager, but of course, it made sense. Out of the six second-year students, only Kaia and Jalene came from dragon-witch families. The rest all had human parents.

"You don't have to worry about the Chameleon Sprites," Jalene said, leaning so she could see Icarus and Adina as well. "We've been getting along with them for centuries. Actually, legend has it that Chameleon Sprites taught witches their first spells."

"Indeed," Professor Avery said with a nod.

Adina twisted her hands. "But I heard that Chameleon Sprites can steal our magic."

"Not steal, exactly," Professor Avery said.

"Then what, exactly?" Wickham demanded. His hands were clenched on his desk.

Professor Avery took a moment, rubbing the back of his neck. "It's more like... draining. Imagine your magic is a constant stream inside of a sink. If you put in a plug, that sink will fill up. Take out the plug, and it will drain. The steam is always there, but it varies in how much you have access to at any given moment."

This didn't seem to reassure Wickham at all, although Icarus leaned back, satisfied. Adina frowned.

It wasn't the sprites that Kaia was afraid of. She'd gone to the Golden Forest twice before and had met a handful of sprites. They were mischievous, yes, and had stolen her favorite pair of shoes. But in the end, they gave her shoes back. They were just little pranksters was all.

"After winter break, you will all learn some basic self-defense skills from Professor Sabelle as well," Professor Avery said.

A chill went down Kaia's spine. Even though she had many cousins who had trained as witches here at the Institute, she'd never heard once of any of them learning self-defense. Were the professors expecting more trouble from Odentia?

But if they were, why would they teach us in the second semester when we're back here? Why not train us at the Golden Forest or even before we left? It makes little sense.

Her hand was back up in the air before she realized what she was doing. Professor Avery paused in his speaking and turned to her.

"Yes, Kaia? Is it important?"

Kaia lowered her hand, fighting not to snap back at him. If it wasn't important, did he really think she would ask now of all times? "What I want to know is how the Institute and Crown have planned to protect us this year."

The professor's playfully stern expression turned somewhat grim. And despite knowing that no Odentian warriors were going to pop out from behind the drapery, Kaia couldn't help but look around, making sure they were alone in the room.

"I understand that you're all no doubt nervous about leaving the Institute again, considering the events of the past two years," Professor Avery said slowly. He focused his gaze on Kaia but then turned to each and every one of the students. "However, I can assure you Odentia will not attack us again this year."

Icarus nodded, sitting up straighter. "No, they won't! My parents have been working with the Odentian king as ambassadors, and the relationship between our kingdoms has much improved!"

Professor Avery turned to him. "Thank you for sharing, Icarus, but in the future, don't interrupt me. Always raise your hand before you speak."

Icarus' cheeks turned red as he bowed his head.

"We didn't think that relations were bad enough for Odentia to send their warriors after us before, either," Kaia insisted, not bothering to raise her hand this time. She didn't care if Professor Avery would reprimand her. "So what is the Institute doing to ensure our safety?"

"But things are better," Icarus insisted. "We don't have to be afraid, Kaia. The king of Odentia has promised—"

"And we all know that people lie, Icarus," Kaia snapped.

Her tone was far harsher than she intended, but right now, she didn't want to apologize for it. Icarus had been wrong last year about Finnegan's intentions. He'd let himself be blinded by this optimism, and she would not put her safety in his hands again... even if he had nearly died protecting her from Finnegan.

Instead, Kaia focused intently on Professor Avery, silently demanding that he answer her question.

"We are taking precautions, yes," the professor continued. "Given the events of the past two years, we have decided it wouldn't be wise to assume that nothing of the like would happen again, and so we have asked various military personnel to accompany all witches on their quests this year."

Kaia's heart beat faster. If they had military personnel attending for the students' protection, did that mean the Institute was worried that there would be further attacks?

Professor Avery held up one finger. "But to be completely clear, this is a precaution only. As Icarus said, the relationship between Odentia and Eldavon has improved. The personnel that will join us will be composed of dragons, witches, and humans. This is in part because of King Sydney's new push to have all three branches understand each other better."

Oh. Oh, that was good. Kaia dug her waterskin from her bag and drank, hoping to erase the sticky feeling in her mouth.

"Professor?" Lena raised her hand.

"Yes?"

"Will we have tents again, or do we get cabins this year? I hate sleeping in tents," Lena added.

Professor Avery shook his head. "We'll be going to an established camp where, yes, there are cabins. The weather at the Golden Forest is much cooler year-round than at the Silent Marshes, and we don't want to catch our death of cold, right?"

He sat on the desk at the front of the classroom and explained what would be expected of the students in terms of behavior and decorum. Kaia could hardly listen. Even though she was grateful they would have additional protection this year, she couldn't help but still feel nervous.

It will go away, she told herself, *once things get back to normal. It will all go away.*

CHAPTER

FOUR

IT WAS difficult for Herja to keep her notebook balanced on her knee as the wagon jostled this way and that, but she somehow managed. The paved trail to the Golden Forest had, apparently, washed out in the summer floods, and the dirt path they ended up taking instead had left many a student with motion sickness.

Wickham is very proud of his peppermint tinctures, she wrote, then scratched her chin with the butt of her pencil. *They help, but not as much as whatever Professor Avery gave us. I wish the wagon would move smoother, though.*

As though on cue, Herja was suddenly jostled to one side. It felt as though she'd just been tossed into the air and landed hard back down. The movement compressed her spine and made her groan. Great, just what she needed!

"I thought the wagons were supposed to make it easier," she grumbled as she stuffed her things back into her pack. She fixed it onto her back before hopping from the wagon.

The trip included five wagons filled with supplies for everyone making the journey and room to sit and relax while moving. Since they had brought no horses or oxen, the dragons were hitched into the wagons, leaving the drivers free to monitor things from the roadside. It also meant they could make better progress, seeing as there was plenty of space to sleep.

Not that it was very possible to sleep.

Herja fell into step behind the wagon. It moved ploddingly, and she considered trying to walk and write at the same time, but that didn't seem like a good idea.

Victor, one human who was accompanying them, jogged up beside her. "Need any help?"

"No, thank you." Herja turned her face away, fighting a blush.

Though he was fifteen, just like the rest of them, Herja couldn't help but think he looked older. In fact, with his black hair and roguish grin, she had decided he was perfect for playing the role of hero in her novel...

Whatever role that might be. It wasn't exactly going as planned.

"If you need anything, let me know," Victor said warmly before dropping back again.

Herja smoothed her black tunic-top, peeking behind her to find Victor had rejoined Lena and Kaia. Kaia wore a beautiful blue dress that made her skin look like rose petals and peaches, while Lena's burnt amber top highlighted the chocolate warmth of her eyes.

Why can't I write like that when I'm actually writing? Herja complained to herself.

But, in truth, she was trying to distract herself. Over the first few days of this trip, Lena and Victor had spent almost all their time together. It made Herja remember how, in extremely rare cases, dragons or witches could be paired with humans during the matching ceremony.

It was obvious how easily they connected with each other... why couldn't that sort of thing be easier for Herja?

A flash of red caught her eye, and Herja lifted her head in time to see Penelope hop onto the back of the wagon. She tucked her fiery hair underneath her cap as she leaned across the wagon tongue to refill her water.

"Sure is hot today, huh?" she asked Herja.

Herja shrugged. "Not really any hotter than yesterday. I think you've just exhausted yourself running around talking to all the military people we've got with us."

Penelope gulped down her water and frowned. "I need to learn more about the training process. Don't you think?"

"I didn't mean it in a bad way," Herja said hurriedly. She winced, recognizing the sulky sound of her own voice. "Sorry, I guess I'm just tired of the traveling... Actually, I wanted to ask you if you think I should try to join the military, too."

Penelope tipped back her cap. "I thought you wanted to be a queen."

"I do. But maybe I should join the military so I can understand international politics better."

"I don't think so," Penelope said slowly. "I think you should only join if it's the best way you can serve the Kingdom. It's not something to do for ulterior motives. You know?"

"I suppose."

Penelope kicked her feet in the air as she leaned against the side of the wagon. It was just her luck that now the wagon wasn't jostling everywhere. Herja bet that if she climbed onto it again, they'd instantly hit a rock... it was amusing to think that this road was conspiring against her personally, though she knew that was ridiculous, of course.

Herja's mind turned back to that novel she was writing. She had decided to just go ahead and write it out of order since it seemed to be impossible to write it in order. Now that they were traveling, the words flowed a lot better, but she still didn't get them the way she really wanted.

Thinking of her book, unfortunately, led Herja to think of other things. The mating ceremony and all those sappy romance things.

Ugh! How was she supposed to not focus on the possibility of romance and instead just let her relationship develop naturally if she kept thinking about romance? That was the one thing none of the adults were any good at. She could ask them how until she was blue in the face, but they only ever told her the same things.

The adults in books were no more helpful, either.

"Pen?"

"Hmmm?"

"I know it's silly to ask, but have you thought much about our mating ceremony?"

Penelope refilled her waterskin again. "No, not much. It's going to happen, but we've got a lot to do before that. And it's not like thinking about it is going to change anything, anyway. Why? Have you been thinking about it? I've seen you spend more time with Icarus lately."

Herja glared at her, her cheeks flaming.

"Oh." Penelope hid a smile behind her hand.

"You're impossible," Herja groaned. She pulled herself back onto the wagon and lowered her voice. "I'm not attracted to girls. That leaves Wickham and Icarus. Even though everyone says that it doesn't have to be a romantic connection, it is most of the time."

Penelope nodded. "I don't really know anyone who didn't eventually fall in love with their fated mate."

"It can't be Wickham, then," Herja said firmly. "He's my friend, and it would just be weird, which leaves Icarus. And I don't really like Icarus, so I've been trying to make myself like him. You know, spending time with him and all that."

Penelope handed Herja a water skin. "I'm pretty sure it doesn't work like that."

"But I have gone from disliking him to being neutral," Herja said. "And we're able to talk now. So it is working like that."

"Yeah, but you can't know he's going to be your mate."

Herja shrugged. She might not know for sure, but it was the only thing that made sense in her mind. "What about you? Who would you want to be your mate?"

"You," Penelope teased, batting her eyes.

At least, Herja thought she was teasing.

Penelope laughed. "Oh, you should see your face! No, not you. Even if you were a witch, can you imagine us trying to work together forever? I mean, yeah, we do pretty good together in a pinch but in normal life? I guess I don't really care who my fated mate will be... I like all the witches, and we get along," she shrugged.

"Right," Herja murmured. This was all hurting her head, but as she focused on her emotions, she found she was in the perfect state of mind to write some of the angsty scenes in her book. She scooted back further into the wagon and pulled out her notebook.

Warm chocolate eyes, she thought, then began to write.

THE SOUND of Herja's pen scratching against the paper, combined with the heat of the sun, made Penelope feel dozy. She hooked her fingers on the underside of the wagon and leaned back, so her weight was on her arms. Ahhh.

Days like this were the best part of the transition between summer and fall. They could get so blazing hot, and yet, compared to the chill nights, they felt magnificent. With the creak of the wagon wheels and the chatter of the other students around her, it was almost like being back in the Fire Watch, napping in the shade while everyone else worked around her.

If only the surrounding chatter wasn't so focused on figuring out the possible pairings with the matching ceremony. There were only so many times Penelope could hear about how Lena might be matched with Xena or Nolen, or maybe Odele.

It was a waste of time. Why should they worry themselves silly about who was going to end up with whom when they had their futures to figure out? It wasn't as though their lives started with their match.

And yet, even Herja had been bitten by the bug! It was all extremely annoying.

Penelope just didn't understand what was with all this obsession. The stars would match them with their fated mate, and then they'd figure out what happens after that. There was no point in being so worried about it.

Though Herja did have a good point... there were only two boys among the witches, Wickham and Icarus, and two boys among the dragons, Nolen and Xena. It was highly unusual. In most years, there was an even boy-girl split among dragons and witches. Four boys and eight girls meant there had to be, at the very least, two girl-girl pairings this year.

More, if any of the boys ended up being fated mates.

Shaking her head, Penelope hopped from the wagon once more. It didn't matter. She could be paired with a boy or a girl; it really didn't make a difference to her. No, she wasn't really attracted to girls, but these pairings also didn't have to have anything to do with attraction!

They were still a couple of hours out from the night's rest stop, so Penelope moved closer to their military escorts. She looked over the sigils on their uniforms until she found a sergeant. He was a big man, easily the tallest of anyone here, with the silver eyes that marked him as a dragon.

"Excuse me, do you have some time?" Penelope asked politely.

The sergeant glanced down at her and smiled. "Of course. What can I do for you, Miss? Er... it is miss, right?"

Penelope nodded. "Yeah. My name's Penelope."

"Baxter. Sergeant Baxter," he said, holding out a hand.

Penelope shook it.

"So. What can I do for you?"

"I was just wondering if I could ask you a few questions about your experience with joining the military. When you joined, what was the process, how your family reacted...?" Penelope asked.

Baxter combed his fingers through his light brown hair. "Well. I joined straight out of the Institute. I'd always been good at defense and combat, and once I graduated, I figured I'd take a couple of years working to serve the Kingdom before I figured out what I really wanted to do. It fit me like a second skin, though, so I stayed."

Penelope's brow furrowed as she considered his words. It was possible to join and then leave again; it was true. Nobody said that signing up meant a lifetime of military service, not in Eldavon, at least.

"And your family?" she pressed.

"They told me that whatever work I did, make sure it was fulfilling and helped others." Baxter shrugged. "Didn't have much else to say about it. Why?"

Penelope sighed. "I'm sure you heard it was our year that was kidnapped at the Silver Springs."

The sergeant nodded, his gaze serious.

"I... decided that the best place for me would be to join the military and protect the Kingdom," Penelope said slowly, though it hadn't been much of a decision at all. She'd just known that was what she needed to do, even though she didn't want to make that choice. "My family always expected me to join them in the Fire Watch. They took the change... hard."

"I see," Baxter said slowly. "So, you were hoping for some advice from a soldier?"

Penelope nodded.

"I'm afraid I can't really help you with your family problems," Baxter said. "But I've always found writing out my thoughts easier than saying them. If you have a hard time communicating with your family, it might work better to write to them rather than trying to say things when emotions are high."

"Thanks." Penelope smiled at him and dropped back, acting as though she needed to tie her shoe.

Writing to her family about this rather than saying it to their faces? She hardly thought that would work... but maybe...

CHAPTER
FIVE

WICKHAM STRETCHED HIS BACK, grateful to finally be done with the walking and riding.

He stood at the edge of the wagons, taking a break from helping to set everything up for a moment. Instead, he gazed at the dense, beautiful forest that they would be camping beside. He had thought the Silent Marshes were amazing to look at, but this absolutely took his breath away.

It was unlike anything he had seen before. The trees were covered in leaves, ranging from every shade of gold, amber, and scarlet imaginable. The air was fresh, warm, and yet not heavy with heat. The deep breaths Wickham took were refreshing, invigorating him despite the weariness of the long journey to get here.

"Oh, it's beautiful," Lena sighed beside him. She clapped her hands. "Can you hear that? I'm sure that's a canary. This is going to be wonderful, don't you think?"

Wickham nodded. He certainly was looking forward to the most calm and restful semester. He hoped that Professor Avery would live up to his threat to keep them all so busy that they couldn't think about the mating ceremony.

I like 'matching' ceremony better, he thought. Unfortunately, the idea seemed to fluctuate in his own mind, and he didn't know exactly how to switch it simply to matching. A *match* held so much less pressure than a *mate* did.

As he helped move their food supplies to the mess hall, a sudden shout caught his attention. Wickham nearly dropped the box of fruit he was carrying, his heart jumping to his throat. But he quickly realized that the shout was one of delight rather than fright. He twisted to find dozens of brightly colored lights flickering around the wagons.

Wickham set the box down as one light shot toward him, and a sound like giggles fluttered in the air. It left behind a trail of powdery glitter as it came to hover in front of his face.

A Chameleon Sprite. It had to be.

The creature was small, only the length of his thumb, with a lizard-like body covered in colorful, iridescent scales. It sparkled with rainbows glinting off the long, delicate-looking wings that kept it aloft. Enormous eyes sat on either side of the creature's head, and a slender tail that was at least half of its total body length curled around the hair.

Wickham held out his hand automatically, and the sprite settled into his palm.

"Greetings, young witch," it said, its mouth moving up and down like a puppet's. The sight looked so fake that Wickham, at first, didn't know how to respond.

But then, of course the sprites, with their lizard-like appearance, wouldn't have the mouth structure to speak human language. It had to be using magic to translate.

"Hello," Wickham replied a little awkwardly.

The sprite giggled and leaped off his hand, fluttering back to the others. There, they gathered into a tall figure. The light sparkled brighter, and then what looked like a human woman stepped from the light. The only way to tell that she wasn't human were the rainbow-colored sparks that shimmered around her.

"Greetings, Sabelle, Avery," the woman said, bowing to the two professors. "Is it time for you to teach your students yet another year?"

"It is," Professor Avery said, sliding an arm around his mate's waist. "How is the forest this year?"

"Oh, same as always. We are excited to see so many this year... But there are so many grown-ups. Do you have adult students now, too?"

Wickham picked up the box again and carried it to the mess hall. Herja soon joined him, shooting a glance over her shoulder at the sprites every few minutes. The professors had moved off to one side, talking with the sprite-woman.

"What do you suppose they're talking about?" she asked Wickham.

He shrugged, loading up another box to carry. "They're probably explaining what happened the last few years. It'll be good to have the sprites on the lookout for anyone who doesn't belong."

Herja squinted suspiciously. "I suppose. I hope they don't cause us any trouble, though. We have enough troubles as it is."

Wickham's heart clenched. What troubles was she facing? He opened his mouth to ask her if he could help... but then thought better. Herja didn't like to be offered help. She preferred to figure it out herself. Even if he wished it could be different.

***

A LIGHT TUG on Kaia's hair made her jump. She whirled to find a sparkling sprite in front of her, hovering at eye level.

"Oh!" Kaia exclaimed, putting a hand to her heart. "You startled me."

"I apologize, young witch." The sprite rubbed its strange little hands together. "I was trying to get your attention, but you seemed lost deep in your thoughts." It inspected her curiously.

Kaia rubbed the back of her neck, self-conscious about being caught out like this. She cleared her throat and put on a radiant smile. "Oh, I was just lost in the forest's beauty, I guess. It's just like I remember."

The sprite landed on a branch nearby, its head flicking from one side to the other, looking rather more bird-like than lizard. "You have been here before then?"

"Yes. I've had many cousins come through the Golden Forest in their second years, and I have occasionally come to see them. It's been a few years, though," she added and touched her curls. "And I looked different back then."

"All of you two-legged ones look the same to us," the sprite admitted. "Two legs, bound to the ground, and your strange hands and that fur on your heads."

Kaia couldn't help but laugh. "So, you can't tell a person who has red hair from a person who has black hair?"

"Colors are meaningless."

"Not to us. It's how we tell each other apart; our coloring, our shapes and sizes. So, you and the other sprites, all having similar coloring and shapes, are difficult for us to tell apart."

The sprite looped its tail around the branch. "So strange."

Kaia shrugged. She hadn't ever considered how differently other species would see the world. "How do you tell each other apart?"

"Taste!" the sprite replied, taking back to the air. It hovered around her and slowly came to land on her shoulder. "And I can taste your fear and sadness, young one. I can help and rid you of this bitterness."

Kaia nearly jumped out of her skin. "How can you taste—"

"How can you not?" the sprite replied quickly.

A weird, twisting sensation filled Kaia's stomach. She wasn't entirely certain she liked that these creatures could see through her defenses without her being able to do anything to stop them. Her emotions were her own. Her fears were hers... she didn't want to burden anyone else.

Kaia lowered her voice. "Please don't tell anyone else. I'm working through some things, but I'm going to be all right."

"I can help," the sprite insisted. "I have asked two of the other witches to allow me to aid them and have been rejected already. Please, let me sweeten your days."

"Thank you for the offer, but I really can't accept," Kaia said, flinching a little as she said it. It was clear that the sprite was distressed by her refusal. "I'm sorry that it affects you, but, really, it's just something that I must deal with. It'll get better soon."

The sprite let out a heavy sigh. "Strange witches."

It took to the air and flew off without another word, leaving Kaia feeling a little exposed. What did the sprite mean by 'sweeten her days'? It had described her pain and fear as being bitter, so it clearly meant to ease those emotions. But how?

Kaia's gaze sought the rest of the sparkling creatures, which were trickling back into the forest. Maybe she could talk to Herja—she'd know what it meant and whether it was safe to accept such an offer.

Was it a trick so that the sprite could drain her magic from her?

It occurred to Kaia suddenly that not only could the sprites use their peculiar magic to make themselves look different, such as the woman that spoke with the two professors, but they could also turn themselves invisible. She shuffled uncomfortably back toward the wagons. Perhaps she could talk to Professor Avery about some sort of charm to make sure that she wasn't being spied on.

As Kaia watched the sprites disappear into the forest, she couldn't shake this strange, shivery feeling. No matter how hard she tried to put it from her mind as she kept working, helping put everything together, she couldn't shake the sense of unease.

When they were finally done, she found Penelope and Herja. There were only a few handfuls of cabins reserved for the second-year students. The military and the two professors would be asleep in tents. Since each cabin had a bunk bed and a single bed, they would be sleeping three to a cabin.

"Let's claim a cabin," Kaia said, "I don't really feel like having to share with anyone else."

Herja looped her arm through Kaia's. "You read my mind."

The three of them quickly went to one of the nearest cabins and put their stuff inside. Herja was fine wherever, but Penelope wanted the top bunk, so Kaia took the bottom bunk, letting Herja have the single bed. Everything was fresh and clean, as though it was magically kept in order, and Kaia sighed in relief as she lay down on the mattress.

"Those sprites are certainly interesting, aren't they?" she asked as she pillowed her head in her arms. She glanced over at Herja, who was already putting out her books on the low shelf beside her bed. "One of them talked to me and said that it could taste my emotions."

"I read they were highly empathetic," Herja replied absently.

Penelope hung upside down over the edge of her bunk, her red hair falling like a curtain toward the floor. "Guess that's why, huh?"

"I overheard one talking to Adina, and it said it could 'take her pain away,'" Kaia said, fighting to keep her tone casual. "What do you suppose that means?"

Penelope wrinkled her nose. "I had one say that to me, too. Herja?"

Herja finished arranging her books and looked up with a distracted expression. "None of them talked to me."

"Yeah, but what does it mean that they can 'take away' our pain?" Kaia pressed.

Herja shrugged.

"How can you not have an idea?" Kaia asked. She straightened, her displeasure clear on her face. Her fingers dug into the mattress; it was harder than the ones at the Institute but softer than the wagon bed.

"Because I don't know everything," Herja replied, sounding offended. "If you want to know, go ask Professor Avery or Professor Sabelle. They've been coming here for years; I doubt that this is the first time the sprites have talked to students about that."

Kaia scowled. The last thing she wanted to do was talk to Professor Avery about this. He had already proven himself strict, and she doubted that he'd have much time to answer questions that he no doubt got a million times before.

"Nah, I'm not that curious," Penelope said.

Herja shrugged. "Up to you. But I wouldn't really trust them. The sprites, I mean, not the professors. They won't hurt you, but they will play tricks... like the nymphs at the Silent Marshes. I actually think they might be distantly related."

She prattled on about her theories, and Kaia responded at all the appropriate times, feigning interest. But she couldn't truly pay attention. Her mind was still on the surrounding forest... and all the secrets it could be holding.

CHAPTER
SIX

PROFESSOR AVERY STOOD by the most magnificent tree Wickham had ever seen. The smooth brown bark was etched with intricate patterns of gold and amber, while leaves every color of a fire hung above them. As a light breeze rustled these leaves, they flickered like flames, giving the illusion that the entire tree was on fire. Warmth exuded from the tree.

Wickham clasped his hands behind his back as he gazed at it, so awed that he felt like a small child in the presence of some ancient power. Adina stood on one side of him, her face rapturous as she gazed up at the tree.

"This," Professor Avery said, laying a hand on the trunk reverently, "is a Phoenix Ginkgo. They are ancient trees. Some believe they can live to be thousands of years old. They produce fruit once every century, and the sprites collect this fruit and take the seeds to spread through the forest. Legend has it, the sun itself planted the first Phoenix Gingko, and from it, all life originates."

Wickham smiled. It was a beautiful notion, even if he knew internally that it was unlikely to be true. How could everything, every plant, and creature, have come from something like this?

But then, they are magical; he thought. *Why can't it be possible?*

"Because of the sacred nature of the Phoenix Ginkgo, we must use certain sorts of magic to harvest wood to make our pages," Professor Avery continued. "In the regular process, paper is made from the byproducts of other things. Sawdust and pulp are collected after logs are turned into planks, scraps, whatever isn't useful for anything else. Our process is somewhat different."

Adina leaned forward, jostling Wickham.

Professor Avery ran a finger down the trunk, a look of concentration on his face. "Open."

The bark peeled back like a wardrobe opening. The professor murmured a few more words, and a wedge of wood slowly eased out of the tree. Professor Avery caught it in one hand, the other pressed against the tree.

Wickham's heart lurched as thick red fluid dripped from the tree's open wound. His hands tingled with the desire to mix a healing poultice. Surely, they weren't meant to cause such ugly damage to a beautiful tree like that?

But Professor Avery placed his hand into the missing chunk of tree and started to whisper words under his breath. To Wickham's amazement and then thrill, the wood grew back, visibly creeping over the professor's hand. Soon, the entire ugly gash was closed, and that beautiful bark covered it again.

"And there we have it," Professor Avery smiled, pulling his hand from the now-healed tree. He shook his hand out, flexing his fingers. "We will practice on other trees for the time being. Once I am satisfied that you have the process, you will be expected to explore the forest with the dragon students, looking for Pheonix Gingkoes to harvest from."

Jalene's hand shot into the air.

"Yes?" Professor Avery asked her.

"Why can't we just use this one?"

"Part of this year's lessons is to grow familiar with the earth beneath you. Witches may not be as in tune with Earth magic as humans are, but we must be aware of its flows and patterns. You will have to use this knowledge to find other trees," the professor answered.

He clapped his hands together. "Now. Lena, Adina, there is a birch nearby I want you to find. Jalene, Icarus, a spruce. Kaia and Wickham, find an apple tree."

Wickham reached over to grab Kaia's hands. A thrill washed through him as his head turned this way and that, searching the trees. He knew what apple trees looked like, even when they were overgrown.

Kaia seemed to be moving a little slower than normal. But when Wickham expressed concern, she smiled happily and said she was just tired. They continued on. Wickham was glad to note that the heaviness of the previous year hadn't spilled over to this semester. Even Icarus seemed more confident in himself like he finally accepted that the others had forgiven him for his part in Finnegan's attacks.

"Wickham, what are you doing?" Professor Avery's voice boomed.

Wickham jumped. He had been kneeling at the base of a large oak, carefully gathering the delicate green lichens that were growing around its roots. He held these up. "Frost lichen, professor. It's very useful in pain management."

Professor Avery frowned at him, folding his rather muscular arms. "I am aware of its uses. But this isn't what you were asked to do. And where is your partner?"

Wickham looked around. Finally, he spotted Kaia some distance away, lying on her stomach with her head on her arms. Heat rushed to Wickham's face as he scrambled to his feet. "Sorry, Professor."

"I understand you are quite the herbalist," Professor Avery continued, his tone still booming as he cocked his head to the side. Maybe that was just his natural voice. "That does not mean you have a free pass to neglect your studies."

"I'm sorry, Professor."

Professor Avery jerked his chin toward Kaia. "Go get your partner and get back to work."

Wickham obeyed, his head bowed with embarrassment. He woke Kaia, who revealed she had found the apple tree while he was collecting his plants.

From there, Professor Avery came over to coach them on how to use their words to open the tree. It was difficult to figure out, and getting the tree to close back over the open wound once he got it was far more difficult than Wickham thought it would be, considering his knack for healing.

Despite these challenges, Wickham found the process soothing. He quickly got into the rhythm of collecting materials, adding his wedges of wood to the pile that Kaia was building—she was proving to be far more efficient than him, even though she kept yawning.

"You're great at this," he encouraged her during their mid-afternoon break. The heat from the sun was lovely, despite the hard work they had been putting in.

Kaia chewed on her snack thoughtfully. "I thought it would be more difficult. I've never had much luck with growing plants before. Even something as easy as daisies I struggled with."

"This isn't growing them, though," Wickham pointed out. "It's word-based magic, and you always have a bit of a knack for words and languages."

Kaia smiled at him. "That's what Madame Adora says. She's my language tutor."

Wickham's eyes widened. He knew that Kaia's parents worked in government, but a tutor? "Whoa. Why do you have a language tutor?"

"Mama and Papa hired tutors for my education because the schloss is far from the nearest city. They decided it would be better to have teachers come to me rather than make me travel miles and miles every day to go to school or live in town away from home." Kaia wiped her hands off. "And I wanted to learn more languages when one of my cousins—he works as an ambassador—was learning to speak Sistaince."

Wickham leaned back against the tree, sipping from his water-skin. There were many children in the village he grew up in who took extra classes in their passions, even a few that had tutors. Mother and Father had discussed hiring one for him when he was younger, but he'd insisted he didn't want one. At the time, he didn't want any more time taken from helping out with his younger siblings.

"Did your parents pay out of pocket, or were they government-funded?" he asked, curious.

"Out of pocket. They could have been government-funded, but Mama and Papa decided that, since we have such a large piece of property that we rent to farmers and the like, there was no reason we should take resources that could go to others," Kaia replied.

Wickham hummed. "And your parents work in the agricultural district, don't they?"

"Yeah. Why?"

"It's just interesting," Wickham said. "You know, I never thought about it much, but your family is pretty rich."

Kaia nodded. "I know. That's why Mother puts her salary into grants to develop more efficient farming practices."

Wickham rubbed his nose. He and his family never went without. They always had their necessities, food, shelter, clothing, and lots left over to take time to relax, have fun, and explore their creativity. He didn't really think they needed more than what they had.

All the same, he wondered—were there others in the Kingdom whom he could give more to?

⊹⊱━⊰⊹

ONCE THE MID-AFTERNOON break and snack were over, Kaia returned to her pile of wood that she had collected... only to find it missing.

She looked around, confused—had she come to the wrong spot? But no, her pack was sitting right where she had left it. She picked it up... only to find it far lighter than it had been before. Her heart slammed into her chest as she opened the pack. *It was empty.* The book she'd brought along? Missing! Along with the additional snacks she had packed.

"Professor!" she screamed, dropping the pack. She looked around wildly, her eyes wide. "Professor! Help!"

Professor Avery was next to her in a heartbeat. The other students gathered around as well, all looking concerned. Kaia fought to keep her emotions in check but couldn't help the frightened tears that welled in her eyes.

"My things have been stolen," she said, her voice pitched high. "It's the Odentian warriors! They've come after us again!"

"Whoa, no, they haven't," Professor Avery said, lifting his hands. "Kaia, deep breaths. There are no Odentian warriors."

"But they stole—"

Professor Avery cut her off with a shake of his head. "That would be the sprites, Kaia. They do this every year. They think it's funny to move around our things and steal our food. I'm sorry; I should have warned you."

Kaia's heart still slammed into her chest, but as she processed Professor Avery's words, it slowed. Of course. They were warned that the sprites were mischievous. It made more sense that they were behind this... after all, why would Odentian warriors steal a pile of wood?

"Let's gather what we have collected into the handcart," Professor Avery said, turning to the rest of the students. "We'll spend the rest of the day processing what we've harvested for the next step in making paper."

He directed the others to work while Wickham lingered nearby, his gaze on Kaia.

Professor Avery addressed him last. "Wickham, please go help Lena and Adina."

"But—"

"Wickham."

Wickham's shoulders slumped, and he shuffled off.

Kaia went around Professor Avery to join in with the helping, but Professor Avery held up a hand. "A moment, please."

"Professor, I'm sorry that I—" But she cut off as Professor Avery gave her a pointed look.

"There is no reason to apologize, Kaia."

"I jumped to conclusions and upset everyone."

Professor Avery sighed. "But are you all right?"

Kaia opened her mouth and closed it again. Even though she knew the Odentian warriors weren't here, she was having a hard time shaking off lingering urges to keep looking over her shoulder. Her hands were trembling, and she felt freezing and tired.

"I'm all right," she said, not wanting to burden the professor. It was silly that she'd feel like this when there was no danger around.

"Kaia—"

"I'm all right," she repeated, this time smiling as she said it. "I had a little fright, but that's over. I should go help the others. Thank you, Professor. But I really am all right."

Kaia skipped off, making sure that none of her lingering emotion was visible. She was the one who always made others feel better... she couldn't afford to let them see she wasn't all right.

I will be, though. All I need to do is get busy and forget about this.

CHAPTER

SEVEN

PROFESSOR SABELLE WALKED through the three pairs of dragons facing off with each other. She would correct posture here and there, though Penelope noted the professor didn't have much to say to Herja. Mostly, she just watched Herja, shook her head, and moved off again.

Today, Penelope was paired with Odele. As they sparred, Penelope kept to her back foot, defending against Odele's punches. The rules were that you could only hit toward the heavily padded torso of your opponent, and each hit won a point.

Odele's lip curled back, her silver eyes narrowed as she danced around Penelope and jabbed her fists at her. Penelope kept up, continually backing away from the punches. Odele was slowing as the fight continued, sweat dripping down her face.

"Why don't you just fight back already?" Odele shouted. She threw her hands into the air, fury, and frustration clear on her face. "We've been doing this for hours, and you just keep toying with me! Stop it!"

Penelope dropped out of her defensive stance, her own eyes widening. She hadn't expected such a visceral reaction from Odele over this! Though she opened her mouth to apologize, her words caught in her throat. What was she apologizing for, exactly?

Professor Sabelle strode over. She wore a sleeveless blue tunic that went to mid-thigh and loose blue trousers underneath. Her hands were tucked behind her back, emphasizing how muscular her arms were as she frowned at the two girls.

"What is going on here?" she asked in her low, monotone voice.

Odele pointed at Penelope accusingly. "She's just playing with me. She keeps getting out of my reach and makes me work harder just to keep up with her, but she won't spar properly. She's not hitting back!"

Professor Sabelle viewed the two of them, her expression emotionless. Eventually, she nodded. "Go to the river. Wash up and cool down. Once you are more centered, come see me."

She turned on her heel and moved to the other students. Penelope rolled her shoulders, scowling. She hadn't even been given the opportunity to explain that she wasn't doing what Odele had accused her of! She glared after her classmate as Odele headed to the river. She didn't want to talk to anyone, so Penelope went the other way.

Unfortunately, it seemed as though she wasn't going to be left alone. A few minutes after heading down the long path to the river, Sergeant Baxter and Victor fell in step to one side.

"It's not fair, you know," Baxter said, swinging his arms. "Playing with people like that. It's not good."

Had the warriors been watching? Penelope scowled at him. "I wasn't playing with anyone."

"You were playing with Odele, there," Baxter said, arching one of his eyebrows at her.

Penelope stopped and turned to him, tossing her red hair behind her back. "I wasn't. I was sparring. She was trying to hit me, and I was concentrating on not getting hit. How is that playing with her? I didn't have any openings to strike back."

Victor snorted. "You did too."

Penelope glared at him.

"Go on ahead," Baxter said over his shoulder to Victor. The younger warrior scowled but started down the path again. Baxter watched him go before he focused on Penelope again. "You know that's not true,

Penelope. You had plenty of openings. I watched you. You nearly took a few blows before you pulled back."

Penelope folded her arms, scowling deeper.

Baxter ran a hand through his hair as he looked up at the sky. "I don't know how dragons are taught, but I know what it's like in the military. You need to learn how to finish a fight. Avoiding blows won't cut it if you ever find yourself in a real fight, one where your opponent is determined to do you harm."

It sounded like he was speaking from experience. Penelope's tight muscles loosed as she realized he must be. After all, it wasn't just an attack on the first-year witches that happened last year. After King Diesel's passing, the Odentian king sent his armies to invade Eldavon.

Penelope had heard little about what happened, only that there was a single clash between the two forces before Odentia retreated. But it occurred to her that Baxter could have been involved in that...

People died in that clash.

"Have you...?" she started but trailed off, not knowing what she wanted to ask.

"Have I?" Baxter pressed.

"I... um... probably shouldn't ask."

Baxter's expression grew softer, somehow. "Are you asking me if I've killed anyone?"

Penelope winced.

"Yes. I have. When you face people who are trying to kill you in the chaos and confusion of battle... you don't have much of a choice."

Penelope shivered. It hadn't truly sunk in before now how dangerous and unpredictable combat truly was. There was danger in the Fire Watch, of course, but even the worst of the wildfires weren't malicious. They weren't trying to kill anyone; they were only acting as fire does.

But in the military, it was different. Even though Eldavon had a peaceful existence, what happened when one of the other kingdoms invaded again?

"So, if I was part of the military," Penelope said slowly. She rubbed her icy hands on her trousers, trying to get rid of the damp feeling, "I'd be sent into battle, too."

"Most likely, yes. Normally we are escorts in diplomatic missions, but the combat has been increasing these last few years... we can hope that Odentia will maintain this new peace, but we can never expect it," Baxter said gently.

And going into battle meant she wouldn't have the option to hold back, not when her life and the lives of her comrades were reliant on her actions. The thought of taking another person's life terrified her, and made her stomach churn. Even hunting and fishing was difficult for her; how was she supposed to...?

"Maybe my family has good reason to be opposed to me joining the military," Penelope murmured.

"It's not a choice to be taken lightly." Baxter tapped her shoulder. "Come on. All the human kids are at the river. You'll have fun with them."

Penelope fell back in step beside the sergeant, her mind turning over what she had just learned. No. It wasn't something she was going to decide lightly. She thought she had already made that choice... but doubts were seeping in. Was it really a good idea after all?

⊰❈⊱

HERJA HAD to chew on her tongue to stop herself from telling Vera about the problems in her stance. Her feet were too close together, making her easy to overbalance, and her elbows jutted out too far, meaning she lost a lot of strength behind her punches.

But Herja had learned long ago that people didn't like it when she told them how to improve.

Vera had overheated earlier in the day, and so the two of them were sparring after class in the evening. The day had been a pretty good one, but Herja was glad to have this time to work on her own sparring skills again.

The only question was, why had Professor Sabelle paired her with someone so obviously behind the rest of the class? Herja had been training her combat skills with Professor Farrow for some time and was more advanced than this. Vera gave very little challenge.

Vera tucked her hand into a fist, her thumb going to the inside of her fingers.

"No, no," Herja said, unable to stop herself. She fell out of her own stance. "Your thumb needs to go on the outside, like this. Otherwise, you could break it."

Vera stared down at her hand. "But didn't Professor Sabelle say we needed to keep it tucked in? Won't the other fingers protect it better?"

"No, because it's curled over to put all the pressure of the punch into your finger rather than your palm. Here." Herja took Vera's fist in her hand and tapped her curled fingers. Not hard enough to hurt, but enough that the pressure would transfer down. "Feel that in your thumb?"

Vera nodded.

"Now, if you have your fist like this," Herja continued, changing the arrangement of Vera's fingers. She tapped again, a little harder this time. "Feel where it goes now?"

Vera opened her hand and, with her other one, touched the areas where the impact had transferred to. "And since this part has more cushioning, it causes less damage?"

"Exactly. Now, let's try this again." Herja smiled encouragingly as she brought up the punching pad.

Vera gave it a lackluster hit.

Herja bit her tongue again. She knew Vera could do better than this. Right now, she was acting awkward and uncoordinated, but last year she was graceful as a swan while moving through the obstacle courses.

"Maybe you're still not feeling well?" Herja suggested, not wanting to be too harsh with her words.

Vera scowled as she pushed her dark hair from her face. "I'm feeling just fine. I don't understand this. I'm supposed to extend my arm but not lock my elbow, and I need to keep my arms in front of me, but these things are getting in the way!"

She gestured at her chest with an even fiercer glare. Though she wore a loose tunic, Herja understood what she was referring to. Vera was almost as big around the chest as Kaia was. While the other girls were growing out, too, Herja thought she was rather... behind in that area.

But I don't even want them, she thought stubbornly.

"I don't really know how to help with that," Herja finally said, rubbing the back of her neck. "Er... have you thought about binders?"

"I... no," Vera said. A confused pucker formed between her eyebrows. "Do you think it would help?"

"Well, you know they're basically just fat. So, the binder would compress and keep them out of the way, I think. I don't know." Herja threw her hands into the air. This topic was rather uncomfortable. She preferred not to think about anybody's body. "Maybe you could talk to the medics about it?"

Vera considered for a moment, then nodded. "Thank you. I hadn't thought about that. Maybe it will help."

"Welcome."

"And..." Vera chewed her lip as she shifted from foot to foot. "Er... could you maybe help me with my form? Professor Sabelle paired us together for a reason. I think it might be because I'm struggling so much, and you're advanced."

Herja's cheeks flooded with heat. She couldn't recall the last time any of her classmates, other than Pen, Kaia, or Wick, had asked her for help. She held her breath a moment, thinking this through. Vera seemed just as embarrassed to be asking, so it didn't seem like a prank.

"I can try," Herja said eventually. She scratched the top of her head, uncertain how to proceed. This conversation had certainly taken a strange turn! "I know I can be a little overbearing at times. If I end up not explaining something well or if I'm throwing too much at you all at once, let me know, okay?"

Vera smiled back, her relief clear. "Oh, I will. Now. What am I doing wrong?"

She took up her stance again. Herja took a moment to remember how Professor Farrow adjusted her stance and mimicked that, getting Vera into a better position. As she worked with Vera, warmth flooded her chest. It felt *good* to be asked for help, and to know how to give it.

If this year continued like this, it would be an excellent year indeed!

CHAPTER
EIGHT

PENELOPE SWEPT up twigs and tiny rocks out of the sparring circles, moving them into a pile for Herja to take to the edge of the forest. Even though they did this every day, the Chameleon Sprites always moved them back. Penelope could see them now, hovering in their little glittering rainbows among the trees, giggling as they watched the three dragons work.

Nolan, Xena, and Vera had a free afternoon, so it was Penelope, Herja, and Odele cleaning up the area today.

"I wish they'd figure out we don't actually like doing this," Odele grumped, shooting a glare at the hovering sprites.

Herja grunted. "I think they do know. It's what makes it funny for them. Whatever it is, they're awfully immature."

Penelope had to bite back a smile at the description of the Chameleon Sprites as 'immature'. They certainly liked to cause trouble, despite them complaining that when the 'two-legged' got angry, it 'tasted bad'. Apparently, annoyance was just fine, but anger was pushing it too far.

"It's better than the brownies in the Silent Marshes, though," Penelope offered. "They get aggressive fast, and then they shoot you with tiny darts filled with a venom that makes you go numb."

Odele shrugged as she filled in a hole the sprites had left. "I guess. I just hope that they don't bother me and Icarus when we go out this afternoon."

Penelope sucked in a quick breath, her head turning to Herja, who had frozen.

"What?"

Odele looked up and smiled in a way that made Penelope think she knew exactly what she was doing. "He wants to look for the Pheonix Gingko, and we're not supposed to go into the forest on our own."

Herja put her fists on her hips. "But I had asked Icarus to let me go with him."

Odelle shrugged. "Guess he didn't want you to."

Oh, no. Penelope pinched her eyes shut.

The tension between students was getting bad. Despite the professors both declaring that everyone would be too busy to think about the upcoming matching ceremony, the sentiment proved to be false. Even when they didn't talk about it, it seemed on everyone's minds. Odele and Herja were especially bad. Herja kept trying to spend more time with Icarus, but Odele was always there, pushing back on it.

Penelope hated it. She hated that nobody seemed to think that they could just be friends without thinking about potential matches. She hated the rampant speculation, how even Kaia and Herja talked about potential matches when they went to the cabin at night.

"I don't think you may speak for Icarus," Herja started.

"I know how he—"

Penelope cleared her throat, interrupting them both. "We're supposed to be working here. If you two want to get into an argument over something that is completely beyond your control, finish your work first!"

Both Odele and Herja jumped and turned to her, their jaws slack. Penelope could understand. Normally, she tried her best to remain impersonal in these sorts of situations. She had interfered in the rising tension between Odele and Herja several times over the last few days.

She was sick of it.

Putting her hands on her hips, Penelope glared at the other two dragons. "I am getting sick and tired of this. So what if you both want to spend time with Icarus? The only reason you can't spend that time together as well is that you're being stupid and turning everything into a competition."

"I am not," Odele spluttered.

"You are too," Penelope said. "What else is this about? You were deliberately provoking Herja."

Odele's cheeks turned bright red as she ducked her head.

"I'm serious," Penelope continued, whirling on Herja as she opened her mouth. "I don't want to hear another word about this! I'm so sick of everyone being obsessed with finding their match."

Herja narrowed her eyes. "It's only natural."

"There's nothing you can do about it! It'll happen when it happens and not before."

"Yeah, but this will be our match for the rest of our lives," Odele insisted.

Herja nodded. "It's weird that you're not more concerned about it. Don't you want to have some idea about who you're compatible with?"

Penelope threw her hands into the air. "That's just the thing! We're all compatible with everyone else. Herja, you would work wonderfully with any of the witches. Odele, same for you."

Both other dragons looked at each other, scowls on their faces.

"You're both thinking about Icarus for some reason, but I've seen the way you look at Lena," Penelope said, pointedly looking at Odele. "And the way you and Jalene are always laughing with each other. As for you," she pointed to Herja, "you can't force it. Look at the way Lena and Victor are always spending time together. Do you think that's going to mean that Victor is her match?"

Herja shook her head.

"Everyone can see that you've set your sights on Icarus, and the reason he's not asking you to go into the forest with him is that you've made him uncomfortable," Penelope said.

Herja's cheeks turned pink, and she fell back a step.

"So, stop making your life and everyone else's miserable with this." Penelope marched to the small shed where their tools were stored and hung up her broom. She might have been too harsh with them, but it was the truth. She was getting so sick and tired of all this constant speculation!

As Penelope started away from the sparring circles, Herja raced after her. Penelope braced herself, waiting for Herja to blow up at her.

"Am I really making Icarus uncomfortable?" she asked instead.

Penelope's shoulders slumped as she looked over at her friend. "Uh... yeah. You are."

Herja wrinkled her nose, deep in thought. "I didn't realize. I'll have to apologize."

Penelope winced. "I'm sorry for blowing up. I should have found a more private place and time to tell you."

"That would have been preferable, yes." Herja turned her face to the sky. "I guess I need to go apologize to Odele too, though, huh? If I've been making Icarus uncomfortable, it means... something to her. I'm not sure, but they are friends. And I have been trying to push her out."

Penelope nodded slowly, relieved that Herja had come to that conclusion on her own. "I'm going to find Wick and Kaia. If you need to talk...?"

"I'll meet you there."

Penelope nodded, feeling miserable now. She needed to apologize to Odele as well, and yet for some reason, that seemed like an impossible task. She hesitated as she looked over her shoulder to where Odele was finishing up the last of the work. Herja joined to help her, murmuring.

In a few minutes, they were laughing.

And then, for absolutely no reason at all, Penelope's eyes burned. A lump rose in her throat, and she turned away, kicking the dirt as she wandered to the mess hall. Kaia, Wickham, Nolen, and a few of the humans were assigned to help the cook today.

She went in and found Kaia and Nolen wiping down the tables while Wickham set them after they were clean. Penelope could use something in her hands, so she grabbed a broom and started coming behind them, sweeping up the crumbs that landed on the floor.

"You don't have to do that," Kaia said brightly.

Penelope shrugged. "Wanna stay busy."

Why was she having such a hard time controlling her emotions? First, the blowup at Odele and Herja. And now she was on the brink of tears? Penelope kept her head down as she worked. She soon found that Kaia's bubbly conversation, punctuated by the occasional grunt of acknowledgment from Nolen, was soothing.

Once they were done, Penelope rolled her shoulders. It was a free afternoon today, so maybe her friends would want to go into the forest and explore. She opened her mouth to suggest it, but Nolen spoke before she could.

"Kaia, I was thinking about going to the apple grove," he said, his voice oddly stiff—not that Nolen was ever not stiff—as he focused on the ground before him. "You want to come?"

Kaia smiled at him... oblivious, Penelope thought. Her suspicions were proven correct when Kaia answered, "Of course! Wick, Pen, Herja, and I were talking about doing a little exploring. We'd love to have you along."

Penelope and Wickham shared a look.

"I..." Nolen said, glancing at them.

"You know what?" Penelope said, a little too loudly, "I'm actually going to bow out. I haven't been feeling great today."

"And I forgot I have some training with the medics," Wickham said quickly. "Actually, Herja was going to come along with me. You two will have fun, though."

Kaia looked a little uncertain... maybe she wasn't as oblivious as Penelope thought. And maybe it wasn't a good idea to encourage this, either. It would only cause more speculation... But Penelope really was too tired to think about exploring. She needed some time alone.

To think.

And maybe, to try and not feel so much.

KAIA'S BASKET was full of apples. If she put any more in, they would bruise under their own weight. She stretched her back as she turned her face to the blue sky. Though the witch students were supposed to be searching the forest for a Pheonix Ginkgo to harvest from, she couldn't bring herself to stray further than the river or the apples.

"It's beautiful, isn't it?" Nolen asked as he set his basket beside hers.

"It is. It's all so yellow and orange and red," Kaia mused. She swept her hands around the fallen leaves. Normally, she would have expected to see the ground littered with fruit, but she knew the sprites harvested all apples that fell to the forest floor. "And it smells crisp and clear and like a forest should."

Nolen's lips twitched slightly. "Unlike the Silent Marshes, you mean?"

Kaia wrinkled her nose as she remembered the flatulent scents that permeated the Silent Marshes. "I guess, yeah. But I forgot, your family is part of the Watch there, isn't it?"

"Yeah."

She leaned against the warm bark of a tree. "We could have used you there last year. After Professor Lee was injured, we didn't have anyone who actually knew the swamp."

Nolen grunted. He did that a lot. "The Golden Forest is noisy. It is beautiful, yes, but I don't like it that much. I prefer the quiet."

"You must hate the way I'm always chattering on, then."

"You don't sound noisy when you talk." Nolen laced his fingers together and put them behind his head, looking upward. "I wish I had been with you and the other witches last year. But the brownies all kept talking about how you and the others were very brave."

"Brownies talk?" Kaia asked, surprised.

Nolen dropped his gaze and nodded.

Kaia hesitated, wrapping her arms around herself. "I didn't feel brave. At first, I thought we were just running and hiding to avoid being kidnapped. Part of me thought maybe we would have been better off going to the Odentian warriors, for Professor Lee's sake."

"But?"

"But... I learned it wasn't true. We were running and hiding because the Odentian warriors would have killed him. They would have killed us all." Kaia shuddered, feeling cold and clammy despite the warm fall day. Her next words were little more than a whisper. "I was so afraid. I'm still afraid."

Nolen stepped a little closer, though he still didn't look at her. "Icarus told me that Finnegan was sentenced to life in jail."

Kaia flinched. "I know—it's silly to be—"

"Not silly." Nolen dropped his hands and looked back at her, his silver eyes glowing. "You're never silly for having emotion, Kaia."

A strange sort of warmth filled her chest. It tightened around her heart, but it didn't hurt. In fact, it somehow made it easier to breathe. What was it? As she stared into Nolen's eyes, though, she found it didn't matter. She was just happy that he was here.

CHAPTER
NINE

WICKHAM CROUCHED, checking how level the dried frost lichen was in the little cup. It was just barely showing over the top, which was just right. He straightened and tipped it into the mortar, then picked up the smooth stone pestle and ground the lichen. The motion was familiar and soothing, especially after spending the day carving woodblocks into chips to make pulp.

"Are you doing this again?" Herja complained as she looked up from her book. She tossed it back into her bag.

"It's ready to prepare," Wickham protested.

Herja stood and stretched her back. "Yeah, yeah, I know that. But you heard Professor Avery. You're supposed to take more time to search the forest and get to know the earth's movements. I'm sure it will help you find more herbs and plants," she added.

Wickham grunted in response. He really wanted to get this powder done today, so he could start prepping the little jars of ointment. They'd be useful to treat the blisters that all the witches had been getting lately.

Kaia had returned with Nolen some time ago, and both of them had rope burns on their hands from scaling a short cliff. If they had

had a potion with them, they could have healed themselves in the forest.

"Hey." Herja poked his cheek.

Wickham lifted his head distractedly.

"I'm taking Adina out into the forest," Herja said, leaning in closer. "Do you want to come?"

"Maybe later," he said.

If she had invited him out just the two of them, he might have been tempted, even though he had a lot of work here. But she was only inviting him because she didn't want to be alone with Adina. Wickham didn't even understand why she'd take Adina into the forest at all.

"You're supposed to be going out into the forest," Herja said.

"Maybe later," Wickham repeated, ducking his head. He didn't want her to see his blush. If she did, it would give him away in a heartbeat.

Instead, he didn't see Herja roll her eyes. He didn't even realize when she walked away.

⊰⊱

"MAYBE LATER," Herja muttered under her breath, scowling at the ground. Since Penelope told her she was making Icarus uncomfortable with her focus, she had been doing her best to spend time with all the other witches too.

In the end, she didn't really like it. Most of the time, she wished Wickham was around. At least he laughed at her jokes rather than giving her a weird look that made her feel somewhat small.

But lately it seemed he was always too busy with his herbs and potions to spend any time with her. Was she really more boring than grinding up dried plants?

Adina was already ready and waiting for her, with Odele and Kaia nearby getting their things together. Herja took a deep breath as she approached and made herself smile even though she wanted to keep scowling.

"I hope you haven't been waiting long," she said politely to Adina.

Adina shook her head. "No, not long. Kaia and Odele are going to search the forest, too. I thought maybe the four of us could stick together?"

Herja glanced at Odele, who gave her a wary look. "If Odele and Kaia are good with it—"

"We are," Kaia said a little too quickly.

Herja stared at her. Was she nervous about going into the forest alone with Odele?

"I just think we'd be better off with more eyes," Kaia said somewhat defensively as she lifted her chin. "After all, the more of us there are, the more likely we'll find the tree, right?"

"Yeah," Odele said, though she was giving Kaia the same half-worried, half-confused look Herja was feeling.

Adina hefted her pack onto her back. "Let's get going, then!"

Her enthusiasm distracted Herja from Kaia's strange behavior. She headed into the cabin, grabbing together a quick pack for herself, and then the four of them headed into the forest. They'd been here at the Golden Forest for just over a month now, and every day woke a little darker and colder. Most of the leaves of the forest were no longer on the trees but on the forest floor.

Odele shuffled along, kicking through the leaves. "I'm always afraid I'll step on a mouse nest when it's like this," she declared.

Herja wrinkled her nose. "Mice won't have their nests up on top of the ground, not when there isn't any shrubbery around to defend them. If there are any around here, they'll have burrowed."

Odele narrowed her eyes at Herja.

"Are there mice in the forest?" Kaia asked anxiously, falling back.

She stared down at her feet; today, she was wearing a long skirt that swished around her calves, paired with high-top boots. The combo looked nice together but wasn't all that practical for the forest.

"There are mice everywhere," Odele responded before Herja could say anything. "They're one of the most prolific creatures. You can find them everywhere, even islands. Sometimes when the ships come across vegetation floating in the sea, they'll catch hundreds."

Kaia shuddered.

Herja moved a little closer. "Are you afraid of mice, Kaia?"

"No. Not exactly. I think they're cute... I just don't want them anywhere near me." Kaia bunched her skirt up in one hand and inched forward, looking wary.

Odele pointed at her skirt. "You should have worn pants. I told you. You'll get that caught on everything."

"We've been here long enough; I think she knows that," Herja snapped, not liking the superior tone Odele was taking with her friend. "Kaia is very used to wearing skirts, and she knows how to walk through a forest. You don't have to tell her the obvious."

"Herja," Kaia protested, sounding surprised.

Odele narrowed her eyes. "I wasn't asking for—"

"Where's Adina?" Kaia interrupted.

Both Odele and Herja jumped. Herja's head swiveled as she searched the surrounding space. Adina was just here.... she couldn't have gone far. Had she kept going, annoyed with their bickering?

"Adina?" Odele called.

"Adina," Herja repeated.

Kaia twisted her hands, shying closer to the two dragons. "Where is she?"

"Adina!" Herja yelled louder. "We won't fight anymore—you can come out."

Silence.

Herja's heart pounded against her ribs. Last year at the Silent Marshes, Adina was the first of the witches who had been targeted. The Odentian warriors had been sent for her specifically. What if the same had happened here? Though it seemed impossible that anyone could have grabbed Adina without them noticing...

Inhaling deeply, Herja forced her guesses aside. "Odele, head back to camp. Inform the professors that Adina is missing."

"But she can't have gone far," Odele said, stepping forward.

"Kaia and I will keep looking for her. But the sooner the adults can get a search party ready, the better." Herja nodded at Odele. "You're faster than I am; you'll get there faster."

Odele hesitated a moment longer like she wanted to argue. Instead, she nodded once and took off back down the path they had come from. Kaia grasped Herja's arm as Odele disappeared among the foliage.

"What if we get separated?" Kaia questioned.

"We won't."

Kaia squeezed her arm tighter. "But what if we do?"

Herja turned to her. Genuine fear shone from Kaia's eyes, bringing Herja up short. As much as she was certain nothing would happen, not so long as they stayed together and monitored each other, it was clear Kaia was terrified.

"Er..." Herja looked around and finally bent down, reaching to unlace her shoe. "Take out your shoelaces. We can tie them together to make a long rope, and we'll tie one end around my wrist and the other around yours."

The shoes felt too big and floppy on Herja's feet without the laces, but once they'd put together their makeshift rope and connected the two of them together, Kaia seemed calmer. She stuck so close to Herja that the rope wasn't necessary as they continued on, but Herja decided not to bring it up. Not yet, at least.

They searched for what felt like hours, but the sun had barely moved in the sky before they finally found Adina. She was sitting in the middle of a little clearing, humming to herself as she braided crowns out of the last flowers of the year.

"Adina!" Kaia shouted.

Adina jumped, looking up. Her eyes widened as Kaia threw her arms around her. "Oh, hello!"

"What do you mean, hello?" Herja barked. The worry that had been increasingly twisted in her gut left her shaky, despite the relief at seeing Adina safe and sound. "Didn't you hear us yelling for you? What have you been doing?"

Adina flinched as she bowed her head. "I'm sorry. I didn't mean to cause you distress."

Herja put her hands on her hips, but before she could question Adina further, Kaia burst into tears. Both the other girls jumped, and Herja's stomach twisted.

"I thought something terrible had happened," Kaia sobbed. She hugged Adina tightly. "Why didn't you answer?"

"I'm sorry," Adina said, flinching. "I guess I got too caught up in the forest's beauty."

Herja awkwardly shifted from foot to foot, uncertain of what to do now. She certainly hadn't expected this sort of reaction from Kaia, no matter how worried she had been. Best to leave any scolding to the adults, then. They probably would prefer it that way, anyway.

"Let's get back to camp," Herja said.

Adina delicately detangled herself from Kaia's embrace. "Yes," she said happily. "Let's get back to camp. I'm sure that all my friends are worried. I would very much like to reassure them I'm all right."

Why was she talking so strangely? Herja frowned at Adina but, given how Kaia was still crying, put it aside. Getting back to camp seemed like the best idea. Maybe if they were fast enough, they could stop the search parties from wasting any time.

THE NEXT FEW DAYS WERE.... Unnerving.

Adina had always been a little reserved, a little cautious. She seemed to stand back and watch things rather than be in the middle of everything. At least, she used to. These days, she was constantly running back and forth, accepting minor tasks and volunteering to help others. She was so... sweet.

And sweet wasn't a word that Herja had ever applied to Adina. Something was definitely amiss, and yet Herja wasn't sure it was something she should complain about. After all, Adina was right here. It was clear she was safe, and nothing seemed amiss except that she was more cheerful and helpful.

It wasn't like the Silent Marshes. There was no sign that Odentia had sent warriors to the Golden Forest, and with as much protection as they had, someone would have known something.

All the same.

Herja couldn't shake the feeling that something was wrong, that there was something staring her in the face that she just couldn't see. And while she didn't tell anyone else, not wanting them to think she was paranoid, she kept a closer eye on Adina.

Your gut is a powerful tool, Professor Farrow always said. And Herja trusted her gut.

CHAPTER
TEN

HERJA STOOD in the middle of the forest, alone, as she listened to the birds call to one another. It was a chill, damp day. She was certain it would start raining soon, which was why she had elected to duck out of training, though she was certain Professor Sabelle was going to be annoyed with her for it.

She hadn't had the chance to leave camp these last few days since Adina's strange disappearance, followed by her even stranger reappearance. Now, though, the threat of rain would destroy any evidence left behind...

"If there is any evidence to be found," Herja grumbled as she turned in a circle. Though she was certain this was the place where they'd lost Adina, she couldn't see anything that gave her an inkling about what had happened.

She walked slowly, shuffling her steps. There were no mice under the cover of leaves, and if there were any, they'd take off long before she ever reached them.... But Odele apparently had made her paranoid. She'd dreamt last night of accidentally crushing tiny little creatures, and the feeling of guilt still sat heavy in her chest.

Soon, she reached the little clearing where she and Kaia had found

Adina. Something was felt off, but Herja couldn't quite put her finger on it.

"Hello," she called. "If there are any sprites around that can tell me what happened, I'd be happy to exchange a few jokes."

She cocked her head, listening, but apparently, the sprites either couldn't hear her or didn't like her jokes. Herja shook her head as she poked around the clearing. Everything was exactly as it had been that day. A ring of bushes outlined the clearing, late-clinging flowers sprouting up throughout the area...

Of course! Herja gasped. These weren't late-fall flowers at all. Pansies, pussy willows, daffodils... these were *spring* flowers.

She dove toward the nearest flower, a deep, velvet-purple pansy, and carefully plucked it. As soon as it was in her fingers, the flower dissolved into glittery dust.

"That's it," she murmured. "This clearing isn't real. The sprites must do something—"

"We must do what?"

Herja whirled and screamed as she stumbled back. The most horrifying creature she had ever seen stood before her. It was easily ten feet tall, with a humanoid face... except instead of a nose, it had a long, pointed beak like that of a heron's. Its body was something like a bird, covered in feathers, but its lower legs were covered in a fleshy scaled pattern with three feet growing from each ankle.

"Oops!" the creature dissolved into a burst of sparkles, revealing a fluttering, buzzing contingent of Chameleon sprites.

One of them inched a little closer. "We got it wrong, didn't we?"

Herja put a hand to her pounding heart. It thrummed in her ears as she slowly processed what had happened. It wasn't a monster she had just faced... the sprites had tried to form a 'two-legged' but the problem was, they mixed up the image of a two-legged person with a two-legged bird!

"You did get it wrong," Herja said, finally catching her breath. She cleared her throat as she lowered her hand. "How long have you been watching me?"

"Is this better?" The Chameleons gathered together again and formed a person who was almost perfect... only it was half a foot tall and had feathers instead of hair and overly large eyes.

Herja squinted at the Chameleons. If they did have something to do with Adina's disappearance, this had to be a trick to distract her... to keep her from finding more clues. Or so that they could kidnap her as well?

"Not really," she muttered, shrugging. "You do a much better job on this clearing."

"We're not doing anything," the little creature said.

If Herja argued, would it push them into coming after her? Herja hesitated before she shrugged, trying to appear casual. "Oh, I guess I made a mistake. I thought you were making a beautiful illusion. Maybe that's what got Adina's attention and why she didn't answer Kaia and me when we were calling her."

The creature hopped forward like a robin rather than walking like a human. "You were very concerned for her, were you not, Dragon?"

Herja squinted slightly, but it seemed a harmless enough question. "Yes, I was. I always worry about my friends when they could be lost or hurt."

"But she was in no danger," the sprites protested.

"I didn't know that."

"We don't understand," the sprites said.

Herja shrugged. "I don't have time to explain."

She turned on her heel and hurried away. The sprites, still as the strange human-like bird, followed her. Their giggling made the hair on the back of her neck stand on end.

They disappeared half a mile from the camp, but Herja didn't trust them not to be lurking in the shadows. She pushed herself faster. A light rain misted down, and she was soaked through the bone by the time she reached camp.

She made a beeline toward Professor Sabelle's tent-office.

"Professor," Herja called as she strode to the opening.

The door flap was open, but she hesitated to go inside. Sabelle was one of the strictest people at the Institute, even more strict than the two headmasters. Professors Sabelle and Avery stood in her office, along with a handful of their military escort.

"Herja," Professor Sabelle said, nodding at her. "So you're not lost after all. Is Icarus with you?"

Surprise rippled through Herja. "Icarus? No. Why?" A horrible thought struck her. "He's gone missing, hasn't he? Just like Adina did?"

"It appears so."

Herja clenched her fists at her sides. "The sprites are behind it. They kidnapped Adina, and now they've got Icarus. They must be draining their magic and doing something to them to change their personalities."

Professor Sabelle nodded at Professor Avery and the military people, and they left the office. "Come in, Herja."

Why weren't they reacting more? Herja frowned as she stepped into the tent, her shoulders tight. "If we act fast enough, maybe we can find Icarus before they drain his magic."

"Why do you think the sprites are behind this?" Professor Sabelle asked, cocking her head to one side.

Herja let out an annoyed breath, then listed everything she had found in the forest. Finally, she ended with the strange encounter with the sprites. "They were obviously trying to distract me," she finished.

"I see," Professor Sabelle nodded. "Thank you for bringing this to my attention. I'll make sure that we look into it further."

That was it? Herja stared at the professor. Wasn't she going to find the sprites and make them tell her exactly what they had done to Adina to make her so giggly and helpful all the time? Herja swallowed, fighting back the angry ball forming in her chest.

"We have to catch the sprites and figure out what they're doing," she stated.

Professor Sabelle shook her head. "I must keep looking for Icarus, Herja. However, if you wish to keep looking into this, I would encourage it. You're a smart girl; I'm sure you can figure out what's going on."

"Why aren't you more concerned?" Herja blew up. "You're acting like nothing is wrong!"

"Because nothing *is* wrong, Herja. I have been coming to the Golden Forest with students for many, many years. There are always a few disappearances, but nobody is ever harmed."

Nobody was ever targeted by Odentia twice in a row, either. Herja had to bite back the words that wanted to flood from her mouth. Clearly, the professor wasn't taking this seriously. Spinning on her heel, Herja marched away. Her hands clenched and unclenched as she tried to work through her emotions.

Being angry meant she would make mistakes. And she couldn't make mistakes. Not when she had to protect the witches...since it didn't seem like anyone else would.

⁓⊰⊱⁓

KAIA LAY IN HER BED, staring at the bottom of the bunk above her. For once, it wasn't emotions that were making her so tired, but rather the effort she had been expending all day. She, Penelope, Nolen, Wickham, and Odele had spent the better part of the day looking first for Herja, then for Icarus. She was glad that it turned out that both had just wandered off, but the day certainly had taken a toll on her.

Although, Kaia had to admit, she found the whole thing unnerving. As much as she knew they had just went for a walk and both were back safe, just like Adina, something didn't sit right.

Maybe it was because of how Icarus had started a food fight at supper, and when Professor Avery scolded him, he only laughed and mimicked the professor. Icarus usually was so serious about things. Kaia couldn't quite figure out why he was acting like this... at least Herja was still her normal self.

The cabin door opened, and Kaia lifted her head, expecting either Herja or Penelope. To her surprise, Adina slipped in. She carried with her a flower crown, the same one she had been braiding when they had found her in the forest.

"Hey, Kaia," she said brightly as she came to sit on the foot of Kaia's bed.

Kaia sat up. "Hi. What are you doing in here?"

"You were acting so sad earlier. I wanted to give you this," Adina beamed. She held out the flower crown. "I know Icarus got potatoes in your hair and I hope that you're not too upset about that."

Kaia smiled. She really could use some cheering up right now... even though she didn't feel terrible like she had grown used to, being tired like this certainly made her melancholy. "Thanks. It's fine, though. I'm not sad, I'm just tired. A good night's sleep will solve all of that."

"Oh. I hoped that you would come swimming with me. It's a beautiful moon out, and the air is shimmering with excitement. Lena and Jalene are coming, too... it might help you feel better." Adina leaned forward and set the flower crown on Kaia's head.

The scent of lilacs flooded the air. Kaia breathed them in, though she must be mistaking the scent for something else. Lilacs didn't bloom this late in the year. "That does sound nice, but I'm tired. We're going to have another busy day tomorrow, too, and I just want to sleep."

"Are you sure?"

Kaia nodded once. "Yes, very sure."

Adina seemed disappointed, but that smile that Kaia had grown very used to these last few days returned quickly. "I hope you have a great sleep, then. Tomorrow is going to be so much fun!"

Kaia laughed. "If you say so."

"I do." Adina stood and waved as she left the cabin.

Left alone once more, Kaia found that she felt lighter than she had before Adina's visit. Adina had gone missing but was back safely. Herja and Icarus were both missing today, and both were back safely. Herja had come back on her own, and Icarus was found napping. Neither of them were hurt.

It meant that it was safe here. The students had plenty of protection. Odentia would not come after them again. Finnegan was locked up; he would not be able to come after her.

Kaia gently removed her flower crown, careful not to crush it, and rolled to her side. The sweet smell filled her nostrils, and she kept one hand wrapped around the crown. The relaxation in her body quickly turned to slumber. She fell into the first dreamless sleep she had had for what felt like months...

All the while, unaware she was being watched.

CHAPTER

ELEVEN

"THERE WE GO," Wickham murmured as he carefully sealed the top of a small glass bottle.

He wiped the sweat from his brow and stepped back, beaming at his collection. The project he spent every moment of free time on was complete. Wickham had enough of these tiny bottles that he could give one to each person in their group. Now, if they felt sick or woozy while in the forest, all they would have to do was mix the bottle of powdered herbs with water and drink it down.

While packing the bottles away, he heard shouting from outside. Wickham jumped to his feet, his heart leaping to his throat.

Bickering had gotten uncomfortably common these last few days, but full-on-fighting? Thoughts flashed through his mind, images of Odentian warriors charging into camp with their swords drawn.

Wickham grabbed his herb pouch and peeked out of the tent, searching for the source of the commotion. He soon found it—Lena and Jalene stood over a pile of hiking gear, screaming at each other.

"You're a bubble-headed idiot!" Lena yelled.

"Better than being a butt-headed buffoon," Jalene yelled back.

Wickham's jaw dropped. Lena and Jelene were best friends! What had happened for them to be yelling and insulting each other like this?

Professor Avery strode ahead as Wickham started forward, intending to find Kaia and help break up the fight. He looked mad. His eyes narrowed, and his cheeks flushed red. Wickham stopped where he was, his stomach clenched.

Oh no. They were going to be in so much trouble.

Neither of Wickham's fellow witches noticed the professor until he was looming over them. Both stopped shouting at once, looking at Professor Avery warily.

"What is going on?" the professor said. His tone, unlike his appearance, was calm.

"I found a Ginkgo leaf," Lena blurted. She held it in the air. "I was out in the forest with Victor and Vera—"

"That's from *my* tree," Jalene snapped. She tried to snatch the leaf from Lena, but Lena jerked back. "I found it yesterday, and I told Lena where to find it. Now she's pretending that it's her tree and that she found it, just because she wants to impress the dragons."

Professor Avery held out his hand. "Let me see the leaf."

Lena hesitated but handed it over.

Wickham inched closer, trying to get a better look. It seemed like the right shape from where he was, but the colors were all wrong. The Pheonix Ginkgo they had seen during the class demonstration was far more vivid.

"That's enough," Professor Avery said sternly.

The leaf quivered. A shower of golden sparks erupted from it, revealing a tiny Chameleon Sprite who buzzed through the air and disappeared into the forest. Both Lena and Jalene shouted in surprise, jumping backward.

Professor Avery made a few hand gestures toward the warriors watching. They gestured back—no, not gesturing. They were speaking to each other via sign language. Wickham watched, fascinated, as he came closer. Professor Avery turned a half-frown onto him, and Wickham froze.

"And where were you during drills this morning?" the professor asked.

Wickham held up one of his bottles. "I was assembling first-aid kits."

Professor Avery shook his head. "Do that on your own time, Wickham, instead of neglecting your studies. Now go help Herja and Odele." He turned his attention, "Lena. Jalene. The warriors will accompany us to where you believe the tree is, but be warned; this seems like more Sprite mischief."

The girls hung their heads and shuffled after him.

Breathing a sigh of relief that he hadn't gotten too much himself, Wickham hurried over to where Herja and Odele were working at the outdoor tables. They were twisting grasses together, making fine ropes. When Wickham slid onto the bench to help them, Herja explained they planned to use the nets to shoo the Sprites away when they had to work in the forest.

"I hope I don't get paired with either of them during the matching ceremony," Odele huffed, watching as Lena and Jalene disappeared into the forest with Professor Avery and the warriors. "They're a little annoying."

"They aren't," Wickham protested. "They just feed off each other's energy."

Odele frowned at him. "They're a bit annoying, is what they are."

"You shouldn't be so judgmental," Herja said in a lofty tone. "After all, the stars will pair us with our perfect matches. We can't decide who they are. How would you feel if your perfect match didn't want to be paired with you?"

Odele scowled. "I'd think that we had a lot of work to do. But I hope I get paired with Kaia. She seems easy to get along with."

Wickham's brows arched. He had noticed that Odele, Kaia, and Nolen had been spending more time together in the evenings, but he had no idea that Odele's feelings went that far.

As he thought about how Odele and Kaia would work together, Herja's hands fell into her lap, and she let out a disbelieving noise. "What about Icarus?"

"What about him?"

"I thought you wanted to be paired with him," Herja sounded affronted.

Odele stared, then burst into laughter. "What, really? Herja, I'm gay! He's a friend. You made a fool of yourself with your jealous act for nothing at all."

Herja's cheeks turned dark red.

Feeling somewhat offended on her behalf, Wickham scowled at Odele. "Don't laugh at her! Our fated mates don't have to be romantic partners, and she wasn't being jealous at all! It's a smart idea for us all to get to know each other. That's what we're here for! You're making a fool of yourself."

Odele's laughter cut out instantly at that. She stared at Wickham with wide eyes, like she wasn't entirely certain she understood what he had said. Wickham slumped back in his chair, glaring at Odele. He had never had reason to dislike her before, but right now, he found he didn't want to spend any time with her at all.

"Wick..." Herja said slowly. "Umm... can we talk?"

Oh no. She was angry with him. He should have kept his mouth shut. His shoulders slumped as he stood, regretting his outburst. Why had he exploded at Odele like that? Herja could deal with her on her own. Wickham knew she didn't like it when other people tried to fight her battles.

"I'm sorry," he sighed, not wanting to leave harsh words hanging over Odele's head. "I shouldn't have said that. It's not true."

Odele pushed herself from the table and shrugged. "Nothing I haven't heard before."

She sauntered off as though she didn't have a care in the world. Wickham sank back into the table and hung his head in his hands. He would have to figure out what made him so angry to avoid that from happening again.

"Wick?" Herja said.

He jumped, having forgotten that Herja wanted to talk to him. Wickham held his breath as he looked at her, dreading what she was going to say.

Herja opened her mouth, then closed it again. It was like she was struggling with something, but what? Wickham stared intently at her—too intently, he realized, but could not stop himself. He wanted so badly to know what she was thinking and wished that it could be as easy as looking into each other's eyes and knowing what the other was thinking.

When her eyes flicked up to his, though, he looked away. No, he wouldn't want her to read his thoughts. They were too vulnerable.

"Odele and I have an understanding," Herja said finally. "We've both agreed that we're far too similar to ever be friends, so we're spending time with each other to figure out what our most annoying features are."

"Sorry," Wickham mumbled, his shoulders still slumped.

Herja started working on her ropes again. "You're always so level-headed... why did you blow up like that?"

"It's the stress," Wickham said at once. It seemed like a good excuse, at least. "When I heard Jalene and Lena fighting, I thought the Odentian warriors had come for us again. I know it's stupid, but that's what I thought. I guess the lingering tension just... blew up."

"Oh."

Herja fell silent once more. What was she thinking? Wickham couldn't bring himself to ask. They worked in silence.

After Professor Avery returned with Lena and Jalene, both sulking after finding out that 'their' Ginkgo was just an illusion, the professor declared they were to spend the rest of the day working on their papers.

KAIA FOUND it both soothing and underwhelming, difficult and yet so boring. She put her hands on the chunks of wood that the others pulled from the trees and whispered, "Become pulp and enter the buckets."

Each time, a tingle of magic would shoot down her neck. Her tongue felt like it was swollen before the tingle ran down her arms, concentrated in her fingertips, and then moved into the wood. Each time, the wood would obligingly disintegrate into the fine, sand-like particles needed for the next step, then lift itself up into the air and settle into the buckets.

Easy.

Clean.

Efficient.

And yet somehow, the lack of challenge was exactly what made Kaia dislike it so much. She couldn't find it in herself to ask for a different position, either. Her own strange emotions were more than frustrating.

After some time, the dragons took a break from their sparring, and Xena wandered over. His short brown hair stood up in spikes over his scalp as sweat dripped down his temples. He smiled as he started to lift the buckets into the wagon for her.

"You don't need to do that," Kaia protested.

"It's no problem."

"So, do you have any plans for tonight?" Xena asked her, resting one bucket against his hip.

He looked at her in that way she didn't like. It was the same way Adina did before she asked Kaia if there could be anything between them when they were in the Silent Marshes. Only Kaia knew it wasn't 'anything' other than a 'romantic something' they were talking about.

Which was odd for Xena, considering that he had never looked at her that way before. Maybe she was reading too much into it. Maybe all this discussion of fated mates was making her think too highly of herself... it was actually comforting, thinking that she was being overly dramatic about the whole thing.

So Kaia put a smile on her face and shook her head. "I was thinking that since we have so much tension around right now, we should try to do something fun all together, though," she said. "Maybe a campfire with the warriors and listen to their stories."

Xena nodded, his silver eyes lighting up. "That would be a lot of fun! Everyone is so caught up in their talk about fated mates and whatever that we forget that we need to be friends first and foremost."

"Exactly," Kaia replied, relieved to hear him say this. Far too much time had been given to the ceremony already. "I'm almost finished up here. Could you grab the rest of that pile there? Then, when I'm done, we can see if the professors will make it an official thing."

"Sure!" Xena nodded enthusiastically. He moved off, and Kaia put her hands on the block in front of her.

"Become pulp and enter the baskets," she told it.

The tingle, swelling, and flow of magic moved its normal path, and the block of wood lifted into the air as it disintegrated into sand. A fireside story time and singing. It was exactly what she needed—what they all needed.

Maybe then this mounting tension would be over, and they could get back to their regular lives.

CHAPTER

TWELVE

THAT NIGHT, when everyone was gathered around, Herja sat as close as she could to the fire. She loved the flames licking up at the sky. She loved finding the subtle patterns and color changes. Unfortunately, during this particular fire, she wasn't so much interested in the fire as she was in the two people sitting across from her.

Though they talked and laughed and roasted sausages on their sticks, neither Icarus nor Adina ate a single bite. They lifted their water skins to their mouths but never swallowed. It was creepy. Herja couldn't even enjoy the stories being told or Professor Avery showing off some magic tricks.

Nobody else seemed to realize how weird they were acting! Even the adults interacted with the two of them normally. Was Herja just being paranoid? Or was there something really wrong happening?

At least Wickham was being normal again. When he blew up at Odele, Herja was worried that he would start being weird, too. But after their talk, he'd gone back to being Wickham. She had even seen him talking to Odele again later on and was certain they had a conversation as well.

As for these two, though... Herja stood and stretched her back.

"Adina, do you mind coming with me to look for some more wood for the fire?"

Adina leaped to her feet at once. "Of course! I'd love to."

"All right, let's go." Herja gestured toward the tree line.

This, in itself, wasn't particularly weird. Last year in the Silent Marshes, Adina had proven to be quite hard-working. It was just this constant, bubbling happiness that made Herja think something was wrong. Adina wasn't the sort of person to wear her heart on her sleeve like this.

"It's been a great day, hasn't it?" Herja said, not knowing where she was going with this but certain she'd figure it out along the way.

Adina nodded, her silvery hair bouncing. "It's been amazing! I was talking with Lena earlier, and she told me she found ants in the cabin. Can you believe it? Ants! They're so funny and cute and hardworking."

"I... didn't think you liked ants."

"Sometimes I don't. But the forest is just so beautiful and relaxing." Adina bent to pick up some branches, and Herja got an idea.

Her heart jumped to her throat, but she acted without letting herself overthink. Herja reached forward and, with a sharp cry, "There's a bug in your hair!" she grabbed a few strands and yanked.

The silver hairs popped out, and Herja closed her fist around them as Adina straightened with a cry, her hands going to the back of her neck. She gave Herja an injured look.

"Sorry," Herja said.

Adina checked her hand, convinced she was bleeding, then offered Herja a small smile. "It's okay."

Herja smiled back and tucked the hairs into her pocket before she went back to collecting sticks. She forced herself to sit through the rest of the stories and songs at the fire until the adults finally said it was time for bed. It was taking all Herja's self-control to sit still.

Penelope and Kaia were slow to get to the cabin. But as soon as all three were inside, Herja shut the door and turned to her friends.

"I know what's going on," she declared as she reached into her pocket. She found the little hairs she'd plucked from Adina's head and pulled them out, then opened her hand to let the rainbow glitter fall through the air. Just as she had expected. "Adina and Icarus are both Chameleon Sprites."

PENELOPE GAZED at the fine rainbow dust; her eyebrows pulled together. What did this mean? Was Herja playing a prank on them? How could two of their classmates just be replaced by Chameleon Sprites?

"They can't be," Kaia stammered, voicing Penelope's thoughts aloud. "They're... them."

Herja lowered her hand. "We have seen the Sprites use their shape-shifting abilities already. We know they like to drain the magic from witches. Adina and Icarus both went missing only to show up again sometime later, acting as though nothing was wrong... don't you find it suspicious?"

"Well... yes," Kaia said slowly. "But—"

"The Sprites have replaced Adina and Icarus. You both must have noticed something weird with them."

Penelope sighed heavily. "Herja. Everyone is acting weird. And I do mean everyone. Even you. You just threw a handful of glitter into the air and said that the Sprites have kidnapped two of our classmates."

"That 'handful of glitter' was a couple of hairs I pulled from Adina's head.

Penelope stiffened. "Why didn't you lead with that?"

Herja's black eyebrows pinched together. "I thought it was obvious."

"Adina tried to make me leave camp," Kaia said suddenly. "It was late, and she tried to convince me to go swimming. Were they trying to kidnap me, too?"

Penelope hurried to her friend and put a protective arm around her. "It's okay. Thanks to Herja, we know now. We have to tell Professor Sabelle right away. She'll know what to do; she's dealt with them before."

"That's a good idea." Kaia shivered all the same. "I'm just going to stay in here, though. You two go warn the professor... I'll make sure nobody has messed with our things."

Why would the Sprites mess with their things? Penelope almost told Kaia that she'd feel more comfortable if they all stayed together in case the Sprites came after her again. But Adina and Icarus' disappearances both happened in the forest. There were protective wards around the camp. Maybe the Sprites needed to lure the witches away from camp to kidnap them?

In any case, Kaia didn't look like she wanted to leave the cabin again. Penelope gestured to Herja, and they slipped out of the cabin.

The darkness of the night made the normally cheerful camp seem ominous. Penelope shivered as she looked around, watching for any signs of the Sprites coming at them. If Herja was right—and Penelope had no reason to think she had lied about this—then how come the teachers hadn't realized something was off? Had the Sprites ever done this before?

Benton and Julie had told her stories about their time in the Golden Forest. They'd loved it. The Sprites weren't dangerous. So why were they kidnapping students?

"Professor Sabelle?" Penelope called as they approached the professor's tent.

Professor Sabelle and Professor Avery were both outside, their arms wrapped around each other as they looked up at the stars. At Penelope's call, they both turned around. Before any of them could say a thing, Adina and Icarus both came rushing from the other side of the camp.

Penelope growled as she shifted into a defensive stance.

"Don't listen to them!" Adina shouted.

Icarus waved his arms over his head. "They're liars!"

Professor Avery arched a brow at them while Professor Sabelle frowned.

"You're Sprites," Herja accused, pointing at the two witches. "You kidnapped Adina and Icarus and replaced them. I know; I pulled hairs from Adina, and they turned into sprite dust!"

"We're not," Adina said tearfully. She clasped her hands together. "Icarus and I were just playing a game. Herja's mad because—"

Professor Avery waved his hand toward them. "The truth," he thundered.

A ripple of magic sparked through the air. It slammed Penelope in the chest, and everything she had been holding in rose up her throat. She clapped both her hands over her mouth to hold it in. Herja did the same, her eyes bulging.

The two forms of Icarus and Adina, however, burst into sparkles. The sound of giggling filled the tent, and a horde of Sprites swept away, speeding toward the forest.

"Really?" Professor Sabelle groaned as she rolled her head back. "They're at it again. Good work, Herja. Apparently, the Sprites have started their shenanigans again."

"The real Icarus and Adina," Herja started.

Professor Avery lifted his hand. "They'll be fine."

"But Sprites drain witch magic," Penelope protested.

"It's neither permanent nor is it painful," Professor Avery replied. "It leaves you feeling a little tired, but the actual process is fairly pleasant. I know, I've gone through it several times," he added with a wry smile. "They probably hide in a pleasant dream. Sprites are empathetic; they don't like to experience pain and sorrow."

Despite Professor Avery's reassurances, Penelope's stomach churned. The thought of the two witches being out there in the forest, lost and alone... made her want to scream.

"There isn't anything we can do tonight," Professor Sabelle continued. "In the morning, we'll start search parties. None of the witch students will leave camp without at least one dragon escort... We'll see if the Sprites will voluntarily release them."

Penelope clenched her fists. "Excuse me? We should go out there right now. We can't just wait around!"

"They're not in danger," Professor Sabelle repeated.

"You can't know that," Herja argued.

"We've been through this before."

Herja snarled aloud. "Then why didn't you realize Icarus and Adina were taken? You're supposed to be protecting us!"

Penelope flinched at her shouted accusation. As upset as she was, she shouldn't yell at their professors like that. She reached for Herja's arm, but Herja yanked away, glowering at the two professors.

"Herja, that's enough," Professor Sabelle said, her voice flat. "It's admirable that you're concerned for your friends, and you are right to question why Avery and I didn't realize the signs. However, it's late, you're tired, and the situation can't be helped with anger."

"But they're out there alone—"

Professor Avery stepped forward. "And they're all right. Regardless of their being kidnapped by the Sprites, they are fine. We've dealt with these situations before."

Penelope put an arm around her friend, surprised when she could feel Herja trembling. This time, instead of pushing Penelope away, she leaned against her. Herja opened her mouth again and then shut it.

"Let's go back to the cabin. Kaia will be worried," Penelope said.

The two girls left the professors. Penelope's mind whirled. This couldn't have happened regularly. She'd never heard about the Sprites kidnapping anyone. With as much time as she spent with other dragons and witches, she should have heard about that... shouldn't she? Penelope scoured her mind.

And she landed on a thought she didn't want to examine. What if the professors were Sprites as well?

They can't be. They were both grumpy all day, and Adina and Icarus have been scarily happy lately. She grimaced as she rubbed her forehead. She should have realized that something was up. Nobody acted that happy all the time!

Kaia was in her bed, her blanket pulled up over her head when they entered the cabin. She started in surprise, then jumped to her feet.

"They said don't even worry about it," Herja spat.

"No," Penelope quickly corrected as Kaia's eyes widened. "They said that the Sprites have done this before, and Adina and Icarus are likely to be fine. And then they said that we'll start looking for them tomorrow."

Kaia shuddered. "They're not going now?"

"No," Herja grumped.

"Because this has happened before, and nothing went wrong. Right? We would have heard about otherwise." Penelope took a deep breath. "In the meantime, we'll be fine. We just have to stay strong and trust the professors. The strength of Eldavon has always been because we can work together."

Penelope smiled in a way she hoped was reassuring. The truth of the matter was she didn't feel very confident in herself. If this had happened before, why hadn't the professors warned them? Why weren't more safeguards put into place?

She climbed into her bunk. "Everything is going to be fine; let's all just sleep, okay?"

Neither Kaia nor Herja answered her.

She was still in her day clothes. Penelope took off her trousers and tossed them to the end of her bed, but her tunic was loose enough to sleep in. She wrapped up in her blanket and rolled toward the wall. Everything was going to be fine. It had to be.

CHAPTER
THIRTEEN

KAIA'S HAIR rustled in the soft breeze as she, Lena, Jalene, and Wickham stood in a small semi-circle in front of Professor Avery. The warriors and dragons were off in the forest, searching for Adina and Icarus. The witches were left at camp, still studying.

Kaia's arms wrapped around her waist as she fought back another yawn. After the fright from last night, she had spent the entire night awake, writing letters to her parents. Only after Herja and Penelope were asleep had she remembered something. A couple of her cousins told her once that they had been kidnapped by the Chameleon Sprites; they had seemed to find the story funny in retelling it.

Kaia was afraid she would end up having nightmares and didn't sleep at all. In the morning, she told Herja what she remembered about her cousins' stories.

The result, however, meant that Kaia was utterly exhausted by this point in the day. Despite the chill air and the water Kaia splashed on her face, she could hardly understand what Professor Avery was talking about.

"Everything produces an energy of its own," he explained. "We have been practicing word-based spells to harvest wood. This involves tapping into the tree's own energy. However, in most cases, we have to pull the energy from our surroundings into ourselves. Otherwise, we might do more damage than good."

Wickham raised his hand. "Like when we're healing people?"

Professor Avery nodded. "Exactly. It takes a great deal of energy and resources to recover from an injury or illness; if we try to heal a person with their own reserves, it might sap them dry."

Lena lifted her hand. "Why doesn't it do that with the trees?"

"Trees have an extensive system inside of themselves. The Pheonix Ginkgo releases a certain magic throughout the Golden Forest. If you tried these techniques anywhere else, the trees wouldn't fare so well." The professor clapped his hands together and looked over the student witches. "This is also the sort of magic that we commonly use for blessings. Would any of you like to volunteer to demonstrate?"

Kaia looked at the others, wondering if any of them thought they needed this... she certainly could use a blessing. But she didn't want to take it if someone else wanted it. When none of the others volunteered, she stepped forward.

"What would you like, Kaia?" Professor Avery asked.

She fought back a yawn as a fresh wave of exhaustion passed over her. "I want to have a sharper mind, so I can help find Icarus and Adina."

Professor Avery's normally stern expression softened. He studied her; then, his eyes swept over the other students. "Is this something we need to discuss further?"

Lena coughed and shifted on the spot.

"Yes," Jalene finally said. "Yes, we do. Even though Professor Sabelle and all of them are out looking, I don't enjoy being here anymore. Why can't we go home? I don't want to be kidnapped and have my magic drained!"

Professor Avery ran a hand through his hair. "I sometimes forget that you don't have the same experiences as I do... The process the Chameleons use to drain magic isn't hurtful at all, Jalene. In fact, there are some witches who come here for vacation, specifically for the experience."

"I don't care. I don't want it to happen to me," Jalene snapped back.

"Professor?" Kaia quickly said, hating that it was her words that caused this increased tension, "I know that a few of my cousins were kidnapped when they were students here, too. Does it happen often?"

"Only when the Sprites are feeling particularly bored," Professor Avery sighed.

"Why would they be bored?" Jalene demanded.

Lena gave her an irritated look. "Why does anyone get bored?"

Professor Avery lifted his hands. "Enough. You should all know by now that the worse the tension is among us, the worse the Sprites' pranks get. They think themselves funny and try to improve the situation for others in the way they would cheer each other up. I know this is worrisome for you, but so long as you stay in camp or with dragons when you go into the forest, nothing will happen to you."

Kaia rubbed her eyes. He was right. It wasn't Odentia. It couldn't be. If Finnegan had escaped and returned to Eldavon to exact his revenge, they would have learned about that long before he had the chance to reach the Golden Forest.

This was normal behavior for the Sprites. Kaia knew that... she had to stop this from getting worse. Jalene and Lena were both twitching even more, the sort of twitching they always had before blowing up at each other.

"Were you kidnapped?" Kaia finally blurted. "When you came to the forest for your second year?"

Professor Avery laughed. "Yes! In fact, I was. Let's sit down; I'll tell you about it."

Relief washed over Kaia as she settled down. Hearing the personal experiences of their professor would have to help... right?

It would help Kaia understand that Adina and Icarus really were kidnapped by the Sprites and not Odentia. And maybe, if she was lucky, she might actually start believing it, too.

WICKHAM SHREDDED a piece of grass between his fingernails as Professor Avery spoke.

"When I first came to the Golden Forest, I was full of nerves, unable to stop thinking about the matching ceremony at the end of the year," the professor started. A fond smile spread over his face. "I was gangly and uncoordinated and had the most awful time trying to attend to my studies."

That sounded familiar. Everyone this year was having the same difficulties.

"One of my cabin mates snored," the professor continued. "It was such a terrible sound. Later, I learned it was because of allergies, but at the time, I had no sympathy. After what felt like weeks of no sleep, I finally took my sleeping bag and went into the forest to sleep. That's when the Sprites kidnapped me."

Wickham tossed his shredded grass away and plucked a fresh piece.

"What did they do?" Jalene asked, her voice wobbling slightly.

"They trapped me in my dreams and showed me a world where everything was perfect," Professor Avery smiled slightly. "Everything went the way I wanted it to. I learned a great deal about magic during that time. When I was rescued from the dream, I was tired but content. Even though it wasn't real, my skills still grew in that time."

Wickham tossed away the second piece of grass. "Why do the Sprites keep kidnapping the students if they know that they'll just have to give them back, anyway?"

"They don't see it as kidnapping, but rather borrowing their magic and giving them pleasant dreams in return. The Sprites aren't wicked; they just have a different way of looking at the world." The professor paused, then smiled. "The thing is, Sprites communally raise their children. They consider these actions as part of their job in raising you lot."

Despite the somber mood, Wickham laughed. He didn't really like the idea of being caught in a dream world, no matter how perfect it was. But he could see the appeal. After the hard year that Adina and Icarus had, they deserved a break from the real world, too.

"Maybe they don't want to be rescued," Wickham said aloud.

Professor Avery laughed. "Sometimes they don't. Now. Kaia, do you want the same blessing or something different?"

"The same," Kaia said, her tone almost overly chipper. Wickham frowned. Was there something else bothering her? "Even if the Sprites are treating them well, Adina and Icarus are missing out on classes."

"Let's sit across from each other, then," the professor instructed. He moved to be seated at an angle from the other students, and Kaia scooted forward to sit in front of him. "Now, sometimes the blessing can be stronger if there is physical touch involved, but it's unnecessary. Would you prefer no touch or for me to put my fingers on your forehead?"

Kaia gestured toward her forehead. "My mother always touches my head when she gives me blessings. I'd like that best."

Avery reached across the space between them and placed his fingertips on Kaia's forehead. Wickham watched intently, trying to feel out the energies of the area. This sort of blessing would be perfect for working with sick people. Two years ago, his father was so sick he couldn't leave his bed for months. Wickham would have loved to comfort him during that time.

"May your mind be clear of what clouds it. May you see things with new breath," Professor Avery said in a low, gentle tone. "May peace and comfort be yours."

Kaia's shoulders dropped at least three inches. Her eyes closed, and instantly, Wickham could see the tension releasing from her body. He stared in amazement; he hadn't even realized that she was carrying so much tension until it drained out of her. She swayed on the spot, her eyes drooping.

Avery caught her by the arm as she almost fell over. "Whoa! Are you okay?"

"Yeah," Kaia sighed, then yawned. "Just... tir—"

Another yawn interrupted her.

Professor Avery helped her to her feet. "Lena, will you please take Kaia back to her cabin? She needs to sleep."

Lena nodded and came forward to take Kaia. Wickham watched them leave before he turned eagerly back to Professor Avery. That sort of magic would be perfect when he was dealing with his patients! Well... patients in general. He did little on his own just yet. But he had seen the healers work, and one of the biggest hurdles to overcome was the stress levels the patients were feeling.

"We won't be learning blessings until the end of the year," Professor Avery said to him, no doubt reading his expression. "To start with, I want you to practice feeling the surrounding energies. Each of you will get a flower seed, and I want you to help it grow."

Wickham held his hand out for his seed, grinning. This was going to be awesome!

<hr>

KAIA SLEPT HARD. She woke up only twice between the time Lena helped her to the cabin and the following morning. Food waited for her beside her bed, so she ate, rolled over, and went back to sleep.

By the time she woke, feeling refreshed, her bladder felt like it was going to burst. She quickly made her way to the outhouse, then joined the other students at breakfast. Nearly everyone else was done, so Kaia ate quickly and then helped Herja and Penelope clean up.

"Have you had any luck finding Icarus and Adina?" she asked them as she put away the dishes after Herja washed them and Penelope dried.

Herja grunted. Dark circles were smudged under her eyes.

"No," Penelope replied. "No sign of them at all."

Kaia turned to her two friends and lowered her voice. "I want to give you both a blessing. I can use my magic to help you see things clearly so that you have a better chance of finding them."

Herja looked up from her dishes. "You don't have the training for that."

"I'm good at word-based magic, and Professor Avery showed us how it was done yesterday," Kaia insisted. "I can do it."

The two dragons glanced at each other doubtfully. Penelope shook her head. "If that would help, Professor Avery would have given us blessings already."

"Like he should have known that Adina and Icarus were replaced from the start," Herja spat. She threw her washcloth into the soapy water and turned to Kaia. "Do it."

Kaia threw back her shoulders, trying to remember the feeling that had swept through her when Professor Avery did his blessing. She put her fingers on Herja's forehead and spoke. "May your mind be clear. May you see what you need in order to save—"

But her tongue seemed to swell too big in her mouth, and she couldn't finish. Something ripped from her. Her lungs froze, and her heart pounded wildly. Her vision tilted, and she collapsed as everything went black.

CHAPTER
FOURTEEN

"HOW COULD YOU?" Nolen snarled.

Penelope rubbed her tired eyes. "Professor Avery just spent the last hour yelling at us for letting Kaia attempt a blessing. We don't need you doubling down."

Nolen threw his hands into the air. "But Kaia—"

"Kaia is going to be fine," Penelope interrupted.

She glanced over at Herja, whose shoulders were slumped and her head hanging. The lecture they had received had nothing to do with her current state, though. Penelope understood her friend too well. This wasn't regret for getting into trouble—Herja was still chastising herself.

The last thing she needed was for Nolen to figuratively beat her up.

Nolen rubbed his eyes. His shoulders were hitched forward, but when he opened his mouth, Penelope cut across him. "We should have known better, yes. We shouldn't have let her convince us to do that, no. But what's done is done, and it's not like we can wave a wand and change what we did."

"You mean what I did," Herja muttered.

"No, what *we* did," Penelope said firmly as she turned to her. "We aren't going to play the blame game, Herja. We made a mistake—I did

as well. I have witches in my family, and I should have known better—
and now we are going to learn from that mistake, not wallow in self-
pity."

Herja lifted her head. "Kaia's still in the hospital."

"She is," Penelope agreed. "But she's going to be okay. We will not
find Adina or Icarus if we let ourselves be consumed by guilt, though.
And you," she pointed at Nolen, "rather than yelling at us, why don't
you go visit Kaia, huh?"

Nolen scowled at her. "I tried—they said she isn't allowed visitors
yet."

"Then keep trying," Penelope said. Her heart was heavy, and she
knew she was acting more snippy than usual, but she couldn't seem to
help it. Penelope dryly reflected on the fact that she seemed to be chan-
neling her inner Professor Sabelle. "I'll do your chores for you if you
want. I know Kaia would like to see you."

Nolen opened his mouth, then closed it again. He flushed bril-
liantly as he ducked his head and shuffled away. Penelope rolled her
shoulders, then turned to Herja. While she thought it would be a good
idea in normal circumstances for Herja to work, to have that distraction from her thoughts, Herja looked dead on her feet.

"You need to go sleep," Penelope told her.

"But—"

"You can't think clearly when you're tired," Penelope interrupted.
She put her hands on her hips and tossed her hair over her shoulder. In
her mind, she suddenly saw herself as Julie; these were actions her
older sister took quite often. Swallowing hard, Penelope softened her
tone. "You're exhausted. Get some sleeping herbs from the medics if
you need it. But you need to sleep."

Herja ran a hand through her short, spiky hair. Without a word, she
turned on her heel and stumbled toward the cabins.

Good. This meant that now the only one who didn't have someone
telling her what to do was Penelope.

It would be easier if someone could be standing right there, telling
her exactly what she needed to do... but she had told Nolen she'd do

his chores. So that was something, Penelope supposed. She yawned as she headed toward the mess hall where the daily chores were listed.

Only when she got there she heard the rumble of a low voice coming from the back of the mess hall. The kitchens were closed at this point in the day, so nobody should be here... Penelope headed back, frowning. Was that Professor Sabelle's voice?

"And I'm saying no. Kaia is one of the few people who can keep Herja in line." Penelope recognized Professor Sabelle's voice.

A high, chirping noise answered. Penelope's heart raced as she froze on the spot. She'd only heard that sort of noise coming from one other being before. But... but this couldn't be what she thought it was. Could it?

Penelope crept to the edge of the kitchen doors. They were propped open a crack, just enough for her to peer inside. Professor Sabelle stood near the prepping counters, her muscular arms folded over her chest. And floating at eye-level was a group of Chameleon Sprites.

"...I know," Professor Sabelle said. "But I'm saying that Kaia and Wickham are off-limits. Herja is a stubborn kid who thinks that she must do everything on her own. If you take either of her friends, she's apt to burn down the forest. It's all I've been able to do to keep her distracted by helping out Vera."

Penelope pressed her hand over her mouth. No. No, this couldn't be happening. No way! That couldn't be Professor Sabelle. The Sprites had replaced her, too...

But if that were the case, why would she be talking to them like this, rather in their own peculiar language?

"Lena is a good choice," Professor Sabelle suggested as the Sprites continued their chirping. "Tomorrow at noon, I'll make sure she's at the river alone."

No.

Sun and moon, help us!

No wonder the professors weren't concerned about the Sprites kidnapping the witches—They were in on it!

꧁ೋ꧂

KAIA HEARD Nolen arguing with a medic as she lay in bed, the heaviness of her lost energy seeping through her. As much as she wanted to just roll over and go back to sleep when she heard Nolen begging to see her, her heart couldn't let it lie.

"I'm awake," Kaia called as she pushed herself up in bed. She arranged the pillows so she could lean against them.

The medic pulled back the curtain, frowning, but allowed Nolen to enter. "Ten minutes, and that's it," the medic warned.

Nolen nodded. "Thank you."

He stood awkwardly just inside the small, curtained-off room. Kaia opened her mouth, then realized she had nothing to say and closed it again. They stared at each other like a couple of strangers.

Finally, Kaia snorted. "This is ridiculous. Come sit down." She pointed at a chair beside the bed.

Nolen's expression was his normal, serious face as he did as directed. He twitched as he held a stick out to her. "Here."

Kaia took the stick, frowning. It had been carved so that one end was slightly more pointed than the other. The other end was bound in leather wrappings. As she ran her fingers along the wood, it conjured an image of Queen Johanna, their witch queen, using a wand as she cleaned up a mess of ink Kaia had accidentally spilled onto the carpet.

"Oh!" Kaia exclaimed. "You bought me a wand?"

"I made it," Nolen grunted.

Nobody in Kaia's family used wands. But then, Professor Avery had said that witches with a higher word-based focus to their magic used wands more than other witches. Her hand closed around the polished leather base, and she beamed at Nolen.

"Thank you. You didn't have to do that."

Nolen shrugged. "Odele told me you're having trouble keeping things focused without touch. Our mother uses a wand to help focus things. So. Yep."

"Thank you," Kaia said again. She ran her fingers over the smooth wood, wondering how long it had taken him to get it so symmetrical.

He grunted again.

"You're allowed to say 'you're welcome,' you know," Kaia teased.

"You're welcome." Nolen looked away briefly before his eyes flickered back to her. "Something else is wrong, isn't it? Something you haven't told the professors."

Kaia blinked. A cold ball ran down her throat to settle in her stomach. Was she being so obvious? She thought she had kept it under control, that nobody else could see the thoughts behind her eyes. Not even Wickham had asked if she was all right recently. Kaia thought that meant she was doing a good job at hiding it.

She forced a smile. "Nothing's wrong."

"If nothing was wrong, you never would have attempted a *blessing* when you haven't even mastered word spells." Nolen folded his arms, his frown deepening. A crinkle appeared between his eyebrows. "You can't fool me. Something else is going on. Tell me."

Kaia found herself bristling against such a direct command. Yes, he was right. But these were her emotions to share or hide. What right did he have to come in here and demand she let down all her walls? His gaze was so intent that it made Kaia uncomfortable, and she turned her face away.

"Please?" Nolen said. "I'm a good listener."

All the air left her lungs, and with it, all her fight. She pulled her knees to her chest and buried her face into her arms. Nolen could be trusted. "I'm afraid."

"Because Adina and Icarus are still missing?"

Kaia nodded.

"Professor Sabelle says that they'll be fine. The Sprites—"

"But that's just it." Kaia lifted her head again. "I'm afraid that it's not the Sprites. I'm afraid that the Odentian warriors have come. I'm afraid that Finnegan escaped from Odentia's prisons... he's the king's brother; maybe they're only saying that he's locked away. Maybe he's going to track us... me... down... and get his revenge."

Nolen leaned forward intently. "Revenge on you specifically?"

Kaia nodded miserably. "At the Silent Marshes, he was always annoyed with me specifically. He only hurt Icarus because Icarus jumped in front of me..."

Memories of the sword swinging toward her flooded Kaia's mind. The coldness in her stomach spread, tingling from her hands. She clenched them, trying to erase the cramping feeling from her muscles.

"I wish I could go back. He warned us, but I didn't take him seriously. I didn't think he would actually hurt us, but he did. He did, and he hates me personally because I wouldn't just shut up. And if he ever comes back...." Kaia shook her head, her words choking off.

Nolen reached for her hand, hesitated, then spread his fingers over hers. "Kaia—"

The curtain was yanked back so suddenly that Kaia and Nolen both jumped. Nolen jumped to his feet, pivoting in the air to face the newcomers. Kaia nearly screamed.

Herja pulled the curtain back shut behind them while Penelope pushed Wickham into the room. He looked furious, a bunch of half-prepared herbs in his hand.

"What is going on here?" Nolen snapped. He put his hands on his hips. "Didn't the medic tell you Kaia needs rest?"

Penelope didn't even look at him as her gaze focused on Kaia. "We have a problem. Professor Sabelle is working with the Chameleon Sprites."

Surprise rippled through Kaia, along with despair. This was the last thing she needed to hear! "You have to be mistaken."

"Professor Sabelle isn't working with the Sprites," Nolen protested.

"I heard her," Penelope insisted. "She was talking to them and said she would make sure they could grab Lena or Jalene—I forget which one—, but she said she was going to help them. She's the one who let them get Adina and Icarus."

Kaia shrank back deeper into her pillows. "There has to be some mistake."

"I thought it was weird that she wouldn't have already known that the Adina and Icarus we've had were fakes," Herja said. Her hands clenched, and her silver eyes glowed with a fury that made Kaia even more terrified. "We can't trust anyone except each other."

"What are we going to do?" Nolen asked.

To Kaia's despair, he sounded fully on board with this. But it was crazy! How could Professor Sabelle know where the other witches were? If she knew, that meant Professor Avery knew. And if he knew... how many of the others knew? Was it all a conspiracy against the second-year students?

Did they do something wrong? Were they being punished? Did the professors intend to replace them all with Sprites?

"I have a plan to make Sabelle reveal her true nature," Herja said, lowering her voice. "But it's going to take all of us. Are you in?"

CHAPTER
FIFTEEN

IT WAS ALMOST DUSK. Herja wrapped her hands in the net that she had woven out of grass. She had thought they would use them as extra protection against the Sprites. Instead, they were using them against their own professor.

We're using them against a traitor, Herja thought fiercely.

Icarus being duped by Finnegan last year was one thing. He was young and inexperienced. Professor Sabelle—*Sabelle*, Herja corrected herself since the dragon didn't deserve the honor of a title—she was an adult. She knew what the Sprites were capable of, and she was still handing over the students as though they meant nothing.

"Listen up, everyone," Penelope whispered. All six of the dragon students and the four witch students left gathered in the cabin. "We're going to have one shot at this. Professor Sabelle is a powerful dragon. If we aren't able to subdue her, we might never figure this out."

"You all know what you're supposed to do?" Penelope asked, looking around at them all.

Everyone looked upset but determined. Herja let out a slow breath, trying to calm herself. It had taken some convincing for Xena and Vera to come around, but Odele had told them she had her suspicions, too.

"Lena, Jalene?" Penelope questioned.

"Yes. We'll distract her while you all get the nets ready," Jalene said. "We've got a big fight we've been saving for this very moment."

The students left the cabin, the tension palpable in the air. They hurried to the various locations that they had decided on. Herja worked fast, remembering all too vividly the events of last year when she and Adina were left running through the swamp with Finnegan and the Odentian warriors on their heels. A kelpie had nearly taken them all out...

They wouldn't have the luxury of help this time, Herja was certain.

In the mess tent, Herja, Penelope, and Nolen set up their net. They moved quickly, unrolling it along the roof while Wickham and Kaia stood guard. When they were done, Kaia lifted her wand, and Wickham put his hand around hers so that they would work together.

"Tangle around the one we wish to trap, and don't let them go," Kaia commanded, and Wickham repeated.

They swayed on the spot as light emerged from the end of the wand. Light shot to the ceiling and spread out along the net with crackling sparks.

Just as Nolen got the two witches into the back, the door opened. Jalene and Lena streaked across the room to hide in the kitchen as Sabelle stepped in. She frowned at Penelope and Herja.

"What's going on?"

Herja lifted her chin, snarling under her breath. Heat burned in her chest, and for a moment, she imagined herself as a gigantic dragon, wings spread and taking up this small space.

"We know what you did," Penelope stated.

Sabelle's eyebrows knit together. "What?"

"You handed Icarus and Adina over to the Sprites," Herja accused. "You were going to hand the rest of the witches over, too. What did they promise you? Wealth? Power? Are you just as corrupt and greedy as the tyrants in the old stories?"

Sabelle's jaw dropped. "What are you talking about?"

"I heard you!" Penelope's hands clenched into fists. "I heard you talking with that Sprite. You were going to lure the witches into the forest for them to take! You're a traitor!"

Sabelle held her hands up. "Girls, you don't understand."

"Why did you do it?" Herja demanded, her voice hard. "Why did you betray our trust?"

"Herja, Penelope," Sabelle started forward.

On cue, Penelope and Herja leaped to their separate sides. They sliced through the rope holding the net in place, and it came down with sparks and flickers of magic. Sabelle cried out, the ropes twisting around her. As she fought to free herself, the net only wrapped more firmly around her.

"Stop this!" Sabelle yelled. "Stop this immediately!"

Herja brandished her fists at the professor. "Not until you tell us where Adina and Icarus are! Not until they're back, safe, and you face your—"

There was only one problem with their plan, as it turned out. Odele and Xena were meant to distract Avery, to keep him away from the mess hall.

Herja's heart sank as the witch professor stormed in. The two dragon students stumbled after him, wincing with bands of light wrapped around their wrists. Avery viewed the scene, grunted, and waved a hand at the net. The magic soaking it faded, and the net fell apart as though the hours of hard work they'd put into it had never happened.

Great. Just great. But this wasn't over.

"We won't let you take the other witches," Herja cried, rolling into a defensive position as Sabelle got to her feet, muttering under her breath. "I don't care if you kill us; we're not letting you—"

"Herja!" Sabelle exclaimed. She seemed so utterly shocked that Herja fell silent. She eyed the professor warily. "What is going on here? Why would you think we'd harm any of you?"

Penelope took up a defensive position as well. "I heard you. For all we know, you're the one who helped the Odentian warriors get to the Silent Marshes last year!"

Sabelle fell back a step, shock on her face. But Herja couldn't allow herself to believe that. Not when Sabelle had spent so many hours working with them. The betrayal pounded at her temples. Avery opened his mouth, but before he could speak, Victor and Baxter stepped into the mess hall.

"Hold up," Baxter said, putting a hand on Avery's shoulder. "Let's all just take a moment to relax, okay? Prof, let these two go. Vera told us what's going on, and these kids deserve an explanation."

Baxter gestured to Xena and Odele. Avery nodded once, and the magic binding them disappeared. The two other dragon students quickly joined the group. Vera peered around the entrance to the mess hall, and Herja had to fight back the urge to shout at her.

The four witches, along with Nolen, came out of the kitchen to join them.

"I had to tell someone," Vera said, her voice high-pitched. "You had to be wrong."

Victor stepped forward. "First off, you all know I'm human, right? If you need to make sure I'm really who I say I am, do what you need to do."

Jalene took Kaia's wand and pointed it at him. "Tell us no lies and hide nothing from us," she commanded. Her words sparked a weak light from the tip of the wand, but the spell dropped to the floor with a damp sort of sound.

"He's Victor," Lena confirmed, taking the wand back. She handed it to Kaia. "I know."

Victor smiled at her, but his expression soon grew serious again. "Before us humans came along, we were told that part of this year's ritual is for the witches to be kidnapped by the Sprites. It's a test of the dragons' resourcefulness to help them understand their roles as protectors. It's been going on for generations, apparently."

Herja's breath trickled from her lungs. Generations? So, Headmasters Twila and Valiant knew about this...

Professor Farrow knew.

And nobody had told her.

"WE'VE SEEN Adina and Icarus ourselves," Baxter added. "Since we have earth magic, the Sprites can't really trick us. We can always see through them. I can assure you your classmates are fine. Professor Avery has been teaching them every evening."

Penelope fell back a step. Her mind churned over this information. Why would they do this? And how come, despite being surrounded by dragons and witches all her life, had she never heard of any of this? She couldn't quite figure out what she was supposed to feel right now.

"I'm sorry that you were distressed," Professor Sabelle spoke, her gaze sweeping over them. "But since this has happened for hundreds of students before you—"

"What makes you think that we're anything like those hundreds of students!?" Kaia erupted.

Penelope jumped. She had never heard Kaia yell before. Her hands were clenched so tight that her knuckles were white. Her face was bright red, and the fury in her gaze was so strong that Penelope backed away from her.

"No other students were kidnapped on Mount Eldavon," Kaia continued. "No other students were hunted through the Silent Marshes. We have been threatened, hurt, hounded, and chased! We have been in situations where we thought we were going to be *murdered!* How can you possibly think that it was a good idea to have us kidnaped again? Why would you put us through that?"

"Kaia," Professor Avery started, stepping forward.

"Don't talk to me!" Kaia screamed. "Nothing you can say will make it better! I quit! I'm going home, and I'm never going to set foot in your classroom again!"

She bolted from the door, hustling Professor Avery aside as she did. Wickham ran after her. Penelope followed, but Herja grabbed her wrist. Penelope glared at her. Kaia needed their support!

But we need answers, Herja's eyes seemed to say. *We need to hear what the professors have to say and decide whether we're leaving, too.*

Penelope took a deep breath and turned her attention back to the professors. They seemed to have a silent conversation between the two of them as well. Guilt and regret were written over their faces... and

Penelope fought against the relief that this sent through her. She still needed answers before she forgave them.

"We're sorry," Professor Sabelle finally said. "We thought it would be best to have this year be a normal one for you. Clearly, we miscalculated. We didn't consider the impact it would have on you."

"We will have Icarus and Adina brought back at once," Professor Avery added. "And from now to the winter break, we'll make sure not to be so insensitive to the trauma you've endured."

Penelope took another deep breath and nodded. "It'll probably be a good idea if we could have therapists come, too. Maybe have the Sprites apologize as well? I don't know if you can make them do that."

"I don't want to talk to a therapist," Herja said. "They don't help. They can't undo the past, just like they couldn't bring my parents back. I'm not talking to anyone! And as for you," she pointed at the two professors. "You just didn't think about our trauma? You're the adults; that's your job!"

Herja stormed off, her shoulders thrown back tight. Penelope recognized the signs... she was about to break down and was embarrassed to have emotions.

They couldn't bring my parents back. Penelope winced. Sometimes she forgot Herja was an orphan. Did that mean that these sorts of things hit her even harder?

Penelope pressed her hands over her eyes, trying to sort through her emotions. No, she wasn't happy about this. No, she would not get over it easily. Yes, she still felt betrayed. But wasn't it better that the adults had acted out of misguidance and ignorance rather than the alternative?

"We are sorry," Professor Sabelle repeated.

"I know. And I know adults aren't perfect... it just could have been handled better." Penelope lowered her hands. "You should have told us, regardless of how things usually are."

"You're right," Professor Sabelle agreed.

Professor Avery nodded. "We'll make sure to send word to all your guardians to explain what happened. And if any of you need to talk...."

"We're available," Baxter said, raising his hand.

Penelope smiled a little at him, but it occurred to her that this was exactly like what was happening with her family. The world was changing. Things were different, and they couldn't just keep pretending it wasn't.

But her experiences were so different from those of her family. They didn't understand... not just why she would join the military but the emotional impact of what she had gone through.

As she left the mess hall to seek her friends and hopefully help them through their emotions, that's all she could think about.

Her experience with life was already wildly alien to her family. So how was she supposed to explain that?

CHAPTER

SIXTEEN

VICTOR LEANED against the trunk of the tree that Kaia sat beside. Even though she was sobbing, he didn't seem to be bothered by the noise. He looked up toward the sky, crooning to himself.

"You don't have to babysit me," Kaia told him between gasps.

Translation: go away and let me cry in peace.

"Who said I'm babysitting you?" Victor replied. His eyes remained locked on the sky.

Kaia couldn't help but glare at him. Even though Adina and Icarus had been brought back, both enthusiastic about their time among the Sprites, Kaia hadn't been able to recover. Professors Sabelle and Avery had told her that if she really needed to return home, they would arrange it. But Kaia didn't trust them to do anything of the sort, not anymore.

The problem was she didn't have anyone to talk about it with. Penelope only tried to justify the whole thing and tried to be calm about it. Herja raged and was more interested in her own anger than anything else. Adina and Icarus didn't think it was that big of a deal since they apparently had been having the time of their lives. Odele, Nolen, Vera, and Xena seemed to have accepted everything. Lena and Jalene would only start complaining; they thought that, since the Sprites led them all to Pheonix Ginkgos in apology, they should have to produce the paper for the witches' spell books as well.

Who did it leave Kaia and Wick to talk to? Just the adults. And she couldn't trust them after what happened!

Victor sat down next to her with a sigh. "You know what I think?"

Kaia glared at him, wiping her eyes. "Go away."

"Uhh... no, that's not what I think."

Kaia blinked at him. Even though it should have been annoying, she had to stifle a giggle. He had an expression of pure confusion on his face, as though he was serious about that being her 'guess'. Kaia took a deep breath and accepted the waterskin he offered her.

"I think you aren't used to being the person who needs comfort," Victor said after a moment, turning his face back to the sky. "That's why you pretend like nothing's wrong until you can run off and cry in private."

"And knowing I wanted privacy meant that you decided to come after me?" Kaia asked, but there wasn't any anger in her tone.

Victor shrugged. "Well, you saved us on Mount Eldavon."

Kaia drank some more water, calming herself. There had been so many children that summer that she couldn't remember all of them. Only a small percentage of them became witches and dragons. Most were human... like Victor. She flinched. He was their age; he went through that experience with them.

"I know the Odentian warriors couldn't be bothered with us humans, but it was terrifying all the same," Victor continued. "It took me a long time to realize that the adults didn't fail us. They had no reason to believe Odentia would attempt to come after us."

"I'm not mad," Kaia murmured. "I'm scared."

It was the first time, besides with Nolen, that she had admitted it. Even now, the confession tasted sour on her tongue as though she was betraying something about herself by saying it aloud. But it also felt good to say it, without getting the expected reaction that she was a witch; it was her job to help others. How could she do that while she was afraid?

"I'm still scared, too," Victor whispered, sharing his secret. "Sometimes I have nightmares. It's why I decided to join the military. I don't want anyone else to be scared like that."

"You're good at it," Kaia said as she leaned back against the tree.

It was the truth... she was already feeling better for having Victor with her. It was strange. Even though they were the same age, he seemed older, somehow. Wiser, maybe. Or maybe, like he could protect her. Even the dragons had learned little combat skills yet. But Victor knew how to use weapons well.

They sat in silence for a long moment. Kaia closed her eyes as the heat of the sun filtered through the treetops. Even though she had declared that she wanted to leave and never return to the Institute, she knew it wasn't true. She would not let her fears overwhelm her. The professors had been extremely gentle with them all these last few days.

Kaia had to admit that she was happy with the few crisp pages she had made from the Pheonix Ginkgo. Once it was bound into her spell book, the pages would be self-reproducing. Every time she wrote one of her spells, another blank page would appear. Professor Avery had advised them to keep these pages safe and to write all the spells they thought of. At this point, the ink would absorb into the pages. But in their final year, they would form pages of their own.

"I don't like crying," Kaia finally said. She wiped her face again. "It's so stupid, and it doesn't help anything."

"I wouldn't say that. A good cry can make all the difference," Victor replied.

And there he was, sounding wise again. Kaia chewed her lip as she considered his words. She always tried her best to be cheerful, to keep a smile on her face as well as everyone else's. "I still hate crying."

Victor laughed. "Fair enough! Anyway, the end-of-semester feast is about to start. I thought you might want someone to sit with during the celebrations. What do you think?"

He grinned at her. And even though Kaia hadn't spent much time with Victor this semester, as she looked into his eyes, a thrill went through her. It was unlike anything she had experienced before. It made her cheeks darken, and her breath caught in her throat.

Quickly, she looked away again. What was wrong with her?

Or was anything wrong at all?

She silently accepted Victor's hand and stood. He talked as they made their way back to camp, and the ease with which he filled the silence made Kaia even more appreciative. Somehow, even though she listened to his every word, it allowed her to think, too.

There were a few things she knew for certain.

One that the happy, simple life she had always thought would be her constant was gone. She would never go back to the life where nothing bad happened; the one where she never had to be afraid of the wickedness of others was gone.

Two, that was okay. Kaia could find strength in this adversity. It was hard. And she could hate it all she wanted. But so long as she didn't let herself be engulfed in those fears, she would be stronger. She'd be able to better help others, knowing those feelings herself.

Three, she wasn't the only one going through this. As easy as it was to focus inwardly, Kaia needed to remember that she wasn't the only person here. Her fellow witches were hunted, too. Icarus nearly died. Adina had been targeted from the start.

Four, she would not forswear the Institute. She was allowed to be angry, and she was allowed to be hurt, but she still had much to learn.

And, finally, she was ready to learn who her fated mate was. More than ready, Kaia was eager. She wanted to know who her forever partner would be. And when she and Victor reached the feast, she looked at her dragon classmates with fresh eyes.

Any one of them would be a good match for her. But who would *she* be the best match for?

After the feast was winding down, several of the warriors pulled out instruments and played.

Victor grabbed Kaia's hand. "Let's dance!"

Kaia reached over and grabbed Herja's hand. "Let's dance," she cried, pulling Herja as Victor pulled her.

Herja's eyes widened, but she reached out and grabbed Odele by the arm. Soon, all the students were in the small area of the field next to the mess hall. Everyone danced with bobbing knees and waving hands. Kaia thought they must look rather ridiculous, but she was having far too much fun to care.

She twirled around and grabbed Herja's hands, dancing with her. "It looks like you and Odele are getting along better," she noted.

Herja laughed. "We made a truce. No more competition until the winter-spring semester."

Kaia laughed again. She spun away, bringing Herja with her. They joined a small group with Xena, Lena, and Jalene. Kaia's eyes skirted over the group, noticing that it appeared everyone was pairing off in loose groups. Xena and Lena danced closer while Jalene and Herja mimicked each other's moves. Odele danced with Adina, Nolen with Wickham, Penelope with Icarus, and Vera and Victor were matched up, too.

Someone's always left out, Kaia thought. *Victor throws off the balance. I don't have a partner; everyone else does.*

But then, the group reformed into a vast circle with no pairs, and Kaia forgot that thought entirely. She threw herself into the dancing, singing at the top of her lungs, spinning and leaping. Sometimes she danced with others; sometimes, she danced alone.

After hours, Kaia stepped away from the group to get herself some water. Her cheeks were flushed with a smile on her face. Though her legs were weighing her down, and she knew she was going to want to sleep all day tomorrow, she didn't want this night to end.

Nolen joined her by the water. "Kaia?"

"Mmm?"

Nolen sipped from his cup, not looking at her. "Are you really not coming back to the Institute next semester?"

Kaia shook her head. Though she had yelled her declaration in front of everyone, she hadn't really thought they would believe her. "No. I'm coming back. I think I just need some time with my family to get through all this. But I'm already doing a lot better than I was."

Nolen gave her a stiff smile. "Good."

"Was there a reason you were asking?" she asked, curious now.

"I... wanted..." Nolen cleared his throat, then downed his water. He turned to her with such a grim expression it made her heart skip a beat. "I wanted to invite you to spend the winter break with Odele and me back home."

Kaia opened her mouth and closed it again. *What?*

"You never got to see how beautiful and restful the Silent Marshes actually are," he said, his tone serious. "I want to show it to you. I want to show you how peaceful it can be. Maybe, if you're able to see that it's not supposed to be like what you went through, you won't be so afraid."

Oh.

What was she supposed to say?

Despite her newfound resolutions, the thought of going back to that place, of facing the trauma she had experienced there, left her dizzy. Even though she knew Nolen was coming from a place of concern, she wanted to yell at him never to suggest that again.

But why should she yell?

It wasn't as though he had a knife to her throat. He was offering; he was saying something that he thought might help.

He couldn't know that the suggestion of going back there left her frozen, her stomach in knots, and the air thin around her.

So, Kaia did the only thing she could do. She smiled and laughed and grabbed his hand to pull him back to the dance. "No, I don't think so," she replied. "My parents and I are going to have a lot of fun this winter. Maybe you should come to the schloss!"

But before he could answer, Kaia danced away. She closed her eyes and let the music embrace her. There was nothing to fear here... and she wouldn't let herself think about the fears that still lingered deep inside her heart.

CHAPTER
SEVENTEEN

WINTER BREAK!

Wickham stood in the common room of his dorm; his arms crossed on the windowsill as he watched the fat flakes drift lazily from the sky. The first snowfall of the year had come and melted away. But now it looked like this snow was going to be thick enough to stay.

He grinned; the gentle crackle of the logs in the fireplace was the only sound besides the occasional flake hitting the window. Wickham always loved the cozy, still feeling that filled his soul when he watched the snow fall. It meant rest to him, the warmth of being tucked away next to the fireplace.

Herja's door opened, and she stumbled out, her black hair a mess. "Morning."

Wickham nodded to her. He had braided his long silver hair as soon as he'd gotten up. It was a habit; he kept it in braids though the night to prevent it from getting tangled. He usually kept it up and out of his face in preparation for the work of the day.

"It's beautiful, don't you think?" Wickham asked over the shoulder, turning back to the snow.

"Yeah. I like how snow looks when it's fresh." Herja joined him at the window, folding her arms over her chest as she watched.

Most of the other students had gone home for the break. But Wickham and Penelope were both staying at the Institute this time, along with Herja. Wickham hated that this would be the first Winter Feast he wouldn't be spending with his family. But he managed to work a few extra hours in the medical wing to buy extra nice presents for them.

"You have any plans today?" Wickham asked Herja finally.

She shook her head. "I was thinking about doing some extra studying, but I might go swimming instead."

Swimming. Wickham shook his head. "You know, it never occurred to me that the pools would be heated and kept open over the winter. I wish I had known last year."

Herja snorted. "I bet there are lots about the Institute you don't know."

"True," Wickham admitted. He turned to her. "Actually, that's something I wanted to ask you about."

"The Institute?"

"No, not exactly—more of things I don't know," Wickham quickly said.

Herja cocked her head and nodded at him to continue.

"I'm not doing well with my worded spells. I always seem to get tongue-tied. And even if I repeat exactly what someone else says, my spells don't work right. But they're a big part of medicine. So, I was wondering if you could help me study and figure it out better."

Wickham held his breath. Everything he had just said was the truth. He was having difficulty with these spells and had started having to take remedial classes. It was another reason he had elected to stay at the Institute over the break.

Another reason, and one he could never tell Herja, was that he and Penelope were worried about her. She had been withdrawn and angry ever since the Golden Forest, and they didn't want to leave her alone. Wickham hoped that by turning her mind to something else, it might help her leave behind whatever was keeping her so angry.

"I don't know how much I can do, not being a witch," Herja said finally. She rested her forehead against the windowpane as she frowned, but it wasn't an angry frown. Rather, it was her 'thinking frown.'

"I know, but the main thing is, I don't understand the process," Wickham explained.

Herja hummed, her silver eyes tracing the falling flakes.

"You're great at figuring out why things work the way they do and what is most important to focus on. I think that's where I'm failing. Professor Avery is helping, but you know me better; you'll be able to figure out what I don't understand easier."

He gave her an encouraging smile. Herja blushed, even though she still didn't look at him. But her thinking frown turned into a smile, and she nodded once.

"I can try, at least. But you remember that I'm not a witch, and there's probably an element of instinct that I can't teach you," she said.

"That's no problem at all," Wickham replied enthusiastically. "Do you want to read through the manuscripts that Professor Avery gave me?"

Herja nodded and turned to the round tables in the common room. "Go get them, and we can start going over them at once. If you're going to be my student, I expect a lot of hard work, Wickham." But she grinned at him, despite her words, and Wickham laughed. She sounded just like Professor Avery!

Several hours later, they had all his texts strewn over the tables. Herja was taking copious notes as they went through each text, debating over what things meant. Penelope, who had gotten up sometime later, came back to the dorm carrying with her a big tray full of breakfast foods. She slid it onto an empty table and picked up a pile of letters. "Wick! You've got mail."

Wickham straightened. It took his eyes a moment to adjust, but he caught the bundle as Penelope tossed it at him. He grinned as he recognized the writing of Mother, Father, Rhett, Donnelly, and even Tara on the envelopes. As he sorted through them, though, he came across one addressed to Penelope.

"Oh, I've got one of yours," he said, holding it out.

Penelope stared at the envelope.

"What's—" Herja started.

Penelope grabbed the envelope and stuffed it into her pocket. "I'll read it later. I'm going to get a head start on my chores." She grabbed a muffin off the tray she had just brought in and headed out. Wickham's hands slowly lowered to the table. He turned startled eyes to Herja.

"What was that about?" he asked.

Herja shook her head. "I don't read minds, Wick. If you wanna know, you'll have to ask Pen. Now let's get some food. I want to finish this chapter."

Wickham put his letters aside for the time being. He hoped he hadn't made a mistake by asking Herja to help him study. She was intense! But then, maybe that intensity was what he needed. Professor Avery told him he got too distracted. Maybe Herja, with her trap-like mind, was exactly what he needed to get him to learn what he needed to know.

THE SCHLOSS WAS A HUGE BUILDING. It was built to be so big because it originally was a government building, a place for various magistrates to gather and discuss the difficulties they were having. However, as the centers of population had shifted, it became necessary for the government buildings to move as well.

Now, since only Kaia, Mama, Papa, and Madame Adora lived at the schloss, it was where all the family gathered for celebrations. And this winter break held many celebrations. Three cousins had gotten married over the year, and five more had had babies. Sixteen people in total would celebrate their birthdays this month, and who could say no to the family gift exchange for the Winter Feast?

"One more round," Kaia begged.

She and a handful of her cousins were playing a card game. Michaela had won every round like she always seemed to do. Kaia couldn't care less about who won and who lost. She just didn't want the fun to be over.

Michaela shook her head, yawning. "It's past midnight, and Mama is going to expect me up to help make breakfast."

Kaia turned to her other cousins, but they were all fighting their sleepiness as well. She sighed as she put the cards away. "All right. I guess it's time for bed."

"Yeah," Peter said as he reached over to ruffle her silver curls. "Especially for you! You turn into a dragon instead of a witch when you don't get enough sleep."

"I would have said a wolverine," Wolfgang said.

Kaia frowned at him. "You mean I stink?"

Wolfgang stuck out his tongue at her. "I mean that you're an adorable bundle of murder."

Everyone laughed, not noticing how Kaia had gone rigid at the word. She managed a smile and quickly bid her cousins goodnight. She retreated up the stairs toward her room. With the rest of the cousins heading to bed, the light stones would be covered soon, and she didn't want to move through the schloss in the dark.

Once she was in her room, Kaia first checked her closet, then her window, and under the bed before she locked her door.

It wasn't paranoia. It wasn't because Wolfgang saying 'murder' had brought up images of Finnegan and that sword again. Kaia was talking to a therapist about this now. She wasn't scared anymore. There was nothing to fear.

⊹⊱✾⊰⊹

KAIA THREW OPEN HER CURTAINS, eager to let the sunshine in. As she yawned, stretching her arms over her head, her stomach dropped. The stick she used to barricade the window was gone. The window was still locked, but where was the stick? She had seen it there last night... hadn't she?

Kaia drew her wand from her nightgown sleeve, but even as she tried to think of the words she needed, she spotted it—lying on the floor, right at the base of the window.

"How did you get there?" she groused, putting her wand away again.

The stick didn't answer. Which, of course, it wouldn't since it was a stick. One of the younger kids had probably knocked it off, and she hadn't noticed because she was so tired. Her eyes had been playing tricks on her. Nothing to be worried about.

Nothing at all.

She pulled on a shirt over her nightdress and headed downstairs. Madame Adora was in the parlor, picking up picture books and muttering to herself. Kaia was amused to see the proper woman's hair hadn't been brushed, her usual white bonnet hanging from her waist.

"Good morning," she called as she stepped into the parlor.

"Oh! Kaia, you startled me." Madame Adora put her hand on her chest.

"Sorry."

"Oh, think nothing of it." Madame Adora quickly donned her bonnet, smoothing her hair back to hide it beneath the fabric.

Kaia thought that her language tutor wore the bonnet because she was insecure about her hair more than anything else. Not that she'd bring it up. The bonnet suited Madame Adora and gave her an air that was both regal and motherly.

"Those kids certainly made a mess in here, didn't they?" Kaia asked as she helped tidy.

Madame Adora tsked. "I had everything put in its place after they went to bed, and I wake up to this. I don't mind them reading at night," she added. "Children should always be encouraged to read. I just wish that they'd clean up after themselves."

Kaia glanced at the clock. Seven. It was far earlier than most of the little ones would wake up. But then, that didn't mean they hadn't been awake during the night. It wasn't as though anyone would break into the schloss just to mess up Madame Adora's hard work.

She shook her head. "I'll talk to Mama about it."

"No need, Kaia. I'll do that," Madame Adora said.

"I will," Kaia insisted. "I'm fifteen now. I should take on more responsibility around the schloss during the holidays. Besides, don't you have family to go visit?"

Madame Adora put the last of the books away. "I thought I might stay for the break."

Stay for Kaia, she meant. Kaia smiled at her. "You should see your family. They'll be missing you."

"Well... perhaps." Madame Adora offered her arm. "Let's go see what your mother is up to, shall we? She was talking about setting up the stars in the grand hall today—and I want to make sure that she doesn't overdo it."

Kaia laughed as they headed off together. The sounds of life were already filling the schloss.

If anyone was here that didn't belong, they would be found before you could snap your fingers. *And*, Kaia reminded herself, *Finnegan is locked away. He wouldn't break out of prison just to ransack the parlor!*

CHAPTER
EIGHTEEN

HERJA RESTED her chin in her hand, studying the move Wickham had just made on the chessboard. It seemed like a mistake to her, but maybe he had a plan that she couldn't see. If he moved his pawn next to the bishop, it would leave the queen a clear path to take out her last rook...

"Are you going to make your move?" Wickham complained.

Or he could just not be paying attention anymore because he was bored.

Herja sighed as she moved a pawn and brought potential danger to her rook. If Herja was right in what Wickham was planning, she would capture his king in two more moves.

"Do you have training with Professor Farrow today?" he asked, moving his queen into a completely useless position.

Herja moved her bishop. "I'm not training with them anymore."

Wickham had been reaching for one of his pieces but stopped with a frown. "Why not?"

Herja scowled at the game. "Because all adults are liars who decided that we shouldn't be told the truth about what was going to happen in the Golden Forest. Because Professor Farrow knew exactly what we were going to get into and decided, eh, they don't deserve a warning."

Herja glared at her king. She had trusted them. She had trusted all the professors, the headmasters, and what had they done? They took that trust and threw it out the window.

"I should have known better," she said aloud as Wickham moved his queen back to where it had been before. "The only person I can trust is me. Everyone else lets me down."

Wickham grabbed her wrist as she moved to make the final blow to checkmate. "So, what, Pen and me are chopped liver?"

Herja blinked. "I didn't say that."

"Ah, so I guess that means that we're not part of 'everybody,'" Wickham said.

"Wick—"

"Which means we're nobody," he continued.

Herja pulled her hand away and picked up the chess pieces. It didn't matter that she didn't officially win. There wasn't anything Wickham could have done to stop it.

"And nobody's perfect...."

Herja frowned at him. What was he getting at?

To her surprise, he grinned at her. "Which means you think Penelope and me are perfect. Awwww, Herja! I never knew that you held us in such high regard."

"What?" Herja leaned back in her chair, flummoxed. How had Wick gone from chopped liver to being perfect? She tried to follow the path of their conversation and only grew more confused. She cocked her head as she studied him. "Are you okay?"

Wickham smiled at her. "Yeah, I'm fine. I just wanted to lighten the mood."

Herja looked down. "I guess I have been kind of... bitter."

"You're taking it too personally," Wickham told her.

Despite the gentleness of his tone, Herja bristled. "How else am I supposed to take it?"

"The Golden Forest is a cherished memory for many witches and dragons—including the Sprites and their abductions," he added. "Avery and Sabelle were just trying to create a sense of normalcy for us. They all were. Even if you don't understand that."

"So, you're on their side now?" Herja huffed.

"There are no sides."

Herja narrowed her eyes. They had talked over what happened in the Golden Forest. But it occurred to her that Wickham hadn't actually done much of the talking. Mostly, he just nodded when she talked and occasionally said something... and she didn't really listen to that.

"Whatever," she grumbled. Even though her immaturity rankled her further, she didn't care enough to stop herself. "There's nothing I can do about it, anyway."

"You could talk to Professor Farrow or the Headmasters."

Herja stood and took the chess set back to the shelf. "Yeah. I could do that."

And they'll just dismiss everything I have to say. I'm not from a magical family; how could I possibly understand? Tears pricked Herja's eyes, but she grabbed the textbooks sitting on the shelf. "Let's get some studying done."

Her thoughts suddenly landed on the notebook with her partially completed romance story in it. She hadn't so much as opened it for weeks now. All her desire to write had gone away. She was too angry to write about love.

Anger passes, she told herself firmly. *Just ignore it, and it will go away.*

At least, that's what she hoped would happen. Because if these awful feelings didn't just disappear on their own, she wasn't sure how to make them go away. You could bake a cake from a recipe. And you could figure out how to whittle with time and instruction.

But emotions? There were no teachers who could tell you what to do with them. There were no therapists who could make them go away.

Only time worked with emotions. Time and pretending they didn't exist.

Great, Herja groaned as she set the textbook out. How am I going to be queen of Eldavon when I'm already Queen of the Angsty Teens?

HERJA AND WICKHAM were studying *again*.

Penelope shook the snow out of her red hair, sighing. She knew they were serious about Wickham getting his word-based magic up to par, but this was getting ridiculous. The reason she had stayed—well, one of them—was that she wouldn't be left alone with her thoughts. If she was going to be ignored all the time, she might as well have gone home.

At least at home, there was a baby she could cuddle.

"All right, that's enough," Penelope said aloud, almost more to herself than to them. Thinking about home only made her wish she had the words to tell her family what was happening in her mind.

She had written something like ten letters already. None of them were good enough; none explained what she was feeling.

Herja looked up. "Enough?"

"Enough studying," Penelope declared. She walked over and stacked up the closed books neatly. She knew better than to close the book Herja was currently reading. "This is our winter break, but you two have been cramming as though it's finals. You're going to burn out if you don't let yourselves let loose."

Relief washed over Wickham's face. He quickly closed his book. "Pen's right. We shouldn't be cooped up all the time. The headmasters checked the pond yesterday. The ice is finally thick enough to skate on. I think that Professor Lee—"

"You go ahead," Herja muttered, pulling her book closer.

Wickham and Penelope glanced at each other. Herja was studious, yes, but she had always known when to take a break before. Penelope had to admit that she was worried about her friend... this wasn't like Herja to close off everything.

"I was thinking it might be nice to go into the village," Penelope offered. She wished Kaia were here. She'd know how to get Herja out of her head. "We could go find presents. The other day, I saw a beautiful snake statue that would be perfect for Professor Farrow's—"

Wickham hissed at her and waved his hands.

Herja gave him an annoyed look. "What's that about?"

"Er... A bug?"

Herja rolled her eyes. "Look, I like studying. I like reading and learning. And I'm not buying Professor Farrow a present. They lied to me and—"

She cut herself off and bent her head over her book again.

Ah. So that was the reason for Wickham's weird behavior. Penelope leaned onto the table, staring intently at Herja. "Nope."

Herja lifted her head. "What?"

"You're not studying; you're hiding."

"Oh, come on—"

"You're hiding," Penelope said again. "You don't study this hard normally. You're mad, and you're trying to pretend like you don't have emotions, and you're trying to act like you don't care that Row and everyone else didn't tell you specifically about the Sprites because you think it was somehow personal."

Herja's jaw dropped.

"Wick and I have been trying to be understanding," Penelope continued.

Even as she spoke, she thought about her own family. Wasn't she doing the same thing? Weren't her letters thrown into the fire, not because she wasn't expressing herself, but because she was afraid of the reactions? Wasn't it easier to pretend like this was personal rather than admitting that everything wasn't about her?

Sometimes you had to hold a mirror to a friend to realize that you were looking at yourself.

"This is bigger than us," Penelope continued. "I can't solve your problems, Herja. I know you didn't ask us to."

"I didn't."

"But the thing about being your friend is that it hurts us to see you hurting. So here's the deal. You like solving problems, yes?"

Wickham shifted from foot to foot, looking between the two girls as though he was expecting things to blow up at any moment.

Herja, however, finally closed her book. "I do."

120

"Then here's the deal. You go talk with Row and figure something out," Penelope said, a plan forming in her head. "And when you've solved that problem, whether it's something that you need to talk to a therapist about—"

Herja growled.

Wickham held up his hand. "How many therapists have you had, really?"

Herja folded her arms. "Just the one. It didn't work."

"So that one didn't work. Did you give up on the obstacle course just because you fell a few times?" Wickham asked.

Herja's scowl deepened.

"Anyway, as I was saying," Penelope said. The other two turned back to her. "You figure that out. And then, I'll share my problems, and you can figure out how to solve them and give me the same treatment I'm giving you now."

Herja's lips twitched. For a moment, Penelope thought she had done it wrong, and Herja would have the opposite reaction to what she wanted. But instead, Herja smiled. Then she chuckled as she stood.

"The same treatment, huh? That means I get to scold and yell at you?"

"I'm not yelling."

Herja waved a hand. "Scold, then."

Penelope nodded once.

"All right." Herja held her hand toward Penelope. "Shake on it."

They shook. Herja chuckled again as she headed for the door, seeming to go talk to Professor Farrow right away. Penelope watched her go, impressed with herself. That could have gone a lot worse.

Wickham seemed to be in a state of shock. "Did... did that just work?"

"Er... I think so?"

"Huh. Okay, that is something new we learned. Maybe it worked because you challenged her?" Wickham ran a hand through his long silver hair.

"Maybe," Penelope said. She shook her head as she put away the books. "I guess I'm just pretty good at this whole friend thing. So, what're your problems, Wick? Maybe I can scold you into solving them, too."

Wickham laughed. "No problems, Pen. None... at all."

But the look in his eyes as he gazed at the door Herja had left through told a different story. One that Penelope thought she understood. Or at least, she understood what the problem was... but she had no way to understand the problems of the heart.

I hope they aren't matched, she thought selfishly. *It would make things so weird.*

CHAPTER

NINETEEN

"I WANT YOU TO KNOW, I would prefer just to ignore everything," Herja said as she strode into Professor Farrow's office. She sat down in the chair across from their desk; her hands twisted tightly in her lap.

Professor Farrow put down the pen they were using and folded their own hands on the desk. "Oh?"

Herja nodded curtly at them. She had gotten close to them since she had moved into the Institute from the orphanage; not only had the professor been the dragons' teacher the previous year, but they had also ended up being Herja's sparring partner, at Herja's insistence.

She had even met their mate. Last winter's feast, they gave her a small present so she wouldn't feel left out.

Row was just the sort of person Herja had once wanted to adopt her.

The thought made Herja's lip tremble. And the flood of sorrow that washed over her made her even more angry. What right did this person have to make her feel like this? She had decided long ago that she was better off unadopted. Herja relied on herself; she took care of herself, and she didn't have to deal with the complications that she saw with the others at the orphanage, the disappointment and pain whenever they weren't adopted.

It's because there's something wrong with me.

No!

She wasn't going down that again! She was better off alone!

Herja jumped to her feet as emotion slammed through her. It built such pressure in her chest that all she wanted to do was scream. Tears burned in her eyes, and she hated it. Hated these feelings. Hated Row for making her feel this way.

"Why didn't you want me?" Herja's voice caught in her throat. No! That's not what she meant to say. "Warn! Why didn't you warn me? After everything that happened, you should have known better!"

Her throat felt rough and sore. She wanted to keep screaming, but that stupid lump was swelling in her throat, and her stupid lungs kept catching.

"You're right."

Herja opened her mouth, but she was only going to start crying, so she quickly closed it again.

Professor Farrow gazed at her with sadness. Their shoulders slumped, and they let out a sigh. "You're completely right, Herja. I should have known better. I know you; I should have known how you would react. I'm sorry."

Herja slumped back into her seat, hiding her face in her hands.

"Change is a hard lesson to learn," Professor Farrow said softly. "I was only thinking about my own time in the Golden Forest. How it was more of a game than anything else because we knew nothing bad would happen. And I was... I was stupid for not seeing that it would be different for you. I'm sorry. And I'm sorry that it took you coming in here to yell at me for me to realize how much you're still hurting."

Herja pushed her face deeper into her hands. This was exactly why you shouldn't try to deal with emotions. If she had just kept ignoring them, she wouldn't be crying right now.

"It's not a lesson that we will be taking for granted," Row continued. Their voice was so soft, so kind.

Why did it make Herja feel even worse?

"We have had several meetings already about how the needs of the students have evolved and what we need to do to address those additional needs."

Herja's hands were pools of tears by this time. She bent lower, hoping to hide, and wiped them off on her trousers. Professor Farrow held out a white handkerchief, and she reluctantly took it. No point in trying to pretend like she wasn't creating a new ocean in their office.

"If you would like," the professor said, "you can join us in the next meeting. It might help you understand what we're doing... and I think it would be a good idea to have the students' input as well. After all, it wasn't until you and Penelope confronted Avery and Sabelle that they realized the impact on the students. It will be good for us to have your voices there."

Herja inhaled through her nose, trying to lessen the lump in her throat. She didn't trust herself to speak but nodded once. Yes, she liked that idea. Maybe she wasn't the right student personally to be in those meetings, but it was a good idea in general.

"Is there anything else you need to talk about?" Row asked gently.

Herja shook her head, too embarrassed. Part of her wished Row would just understand what she didn't say and reassure her that there wasn't anything wrong with her, even though she knew that was impossible.

"Thank you for coming to talk with me. I know it can't be easy to build up the courage."

Herja cleared her throat. "Penelope made me."

Row chuckled. "She's a good friend. Now. There is one more thing that, in full transparency, I should talk to you about."

Herja's heart thumped. She looked up, uncertain.

"I would like to write to Mr. Bryce at the orphanage to see if I can access your mental health records," Row said, looking into her eyes. "But I won't do it if you don't want me to."

A shiver ran down Herja's spine. "Why?"

"I know you've refused to speak to the counselors here at the Institute. I think that if I could see your records, it might help me figure out what sort of approach we need to take with your mental health here at the Institute," Row said.

They looked a little uncertain as they spoke, something which surprised Herja. Row always seemed to know exactly what they were doing.

"But... why do you care?"

"Because I care about you, Herja, and I'm worried for you."

Herja's heart leaped, no matter how hard she tried to smash it back down. Of course they were worried. They were a teacher here; they were worried about all their students.

She nodded, once more unable to trust her voice.

"Thank you. And if you need to talk or even if you need to yell, I'm here, Herja." Row smiled at her.

Herja managed to smile back. They cared because she was a student. She wasn't special. If it had been any other student, Professor Farrow would have treated them just as kindly. No doubt they were looking into Wickham and Penelope's mental health as well. They probably kept in correspondence with all the students' guardians.

She wasn't special.

But she *felt* special.

Maybe even special enough to still have hope of being adopted.

HERJA LOOKED MUCH CALMER and more relaxed when she returned to the dorms. Wickham and Penelope had grown nervous about her long absence and, to burn off that energy, had turned their attention to cleaning the common room.

Wickham held his breath as Herja walked in. Her eyes were puffy and a little red from crying still, but when she smiled at them, they looked genuine. Relief washed through him, making him breathe a little easier.

"Did you talk?" he asked all the same.

"We had an endless talk," Herja said, bobbing her head. "Row is going to get my mental health records from the orphanage and help me find a better therapist, someone who can help me properly."

She wandered to the overstuffed chairs near the fire and sank into them. Though she looked far more relaxed than she had for quite a while, she also seemed exhausted.

"I'm glad," Penelope smiled. She hung the broom back on its hook and stretched her back out. "I was getting worried that I had made things worse."

Herja pulled her knees to her chest and shook her head. "It was a good thing. Now. What's your problem?"

Wickham hid a smile as he turned away. If Penelope had thought Herja would forget about that part of their deal, she should have known better. Herja's mind was an iron trap. Once you told her something, it was there to stay. It was like a superpower.

Penelope cleared her throat and waved a hand. "It's not important."

"Hmmmmm. No," Herja said with an edge of teasing in her tone. "That's not acceptable. You had no problem telling me what to do, so it's my turn to tell you what to do. Sit down and talk to me."

Penelope rolled her eyes but did as she was told. Wickham joined them; this should be interesting. He wasn't entirely certain he wouldn't need to intervene yet, either. Though Pen and Herja got along surprisingly well, that didn't mean one couldn't push the other too far.

Especially since emotions were clearly running high.

Still, they were handling things well so far. Wickham had seen adults lose their tempers more easily than these two, even in the strained circumstances they had found themselves in. *There's got to be a lesson in there somewhere.*

"My problem." Penelope fidgeted, smoothing a wrinkle in her tunic.

Herja nodded encouragingly.

"My problem is the same problem I've had all year. My family and my lack of communication with them. I think I have things figured out, but then I always talk myself out of doing what I need to do."

Wickham frowned. "What do you think you need to do?"

Penelope narrowed her eyes at him. "Excuse me; this is Herja's problem to solve."

"Wick's a good sounding board," Herja replied without missing a beat. She smirked at Penelope, clearly pleased with herself.

Wickham chewed his lip, fighting to keep his eyes from lingering too long on Herja. She was wearing a light blue tunic today, and the color set off her dark eyes beautifully. The way she held herself had so much confidence that it took his breath away.

Herja was so smart. So incredibly knowledgeable. Not only that, but her independence was astounding. Wickham couldn't imagine anyone else their age who could do the things she did. Just look at how she came up with that plan to capture Professor Sabelle! Yes, they were wrong, and no, it didn't exactly work... but if Vera hadn't ratted them out, it would have.

Penelope spoke, and Wickham shook himself. Despite his efforts, he had been staring. Great. What if Herja noticed? But it appeared she was too caught up in Penelope's story to have paid attention to him.

"I know I need to write to my family and tell them about how everything we've been through affected me," Penelope said. "I know I need to tell them that, like it or not, our world is changing."

Wickham let out a breath. It certainly was changing. "But they have to know that."

"Logically, yes. But I don't think they understand how much," Penelope explained. "We haven't had the threat of invasion for so long; they can't remember a time when they had that fear. But now that we have faced an actual invasion, rather than just a threat, they need to understand that my world differs from theirs."

Herja nodded a thoughtful frown on her face. "So, what's stopping you from telling them, then?"

Penelope slumped in her chair. "I don't know. The wrong words, maybe. Maybe because I hope everything will go back to normal and I won't have to. What do you think?"

"I think..." Herja tucked her chin into her hand. "I think we should get a pen and paper and get it written down. The longer you try to make things perfect, the more difficult the task is."

"I've got some extra paper," Wickham volunteered. He quickly left to get it, all the while beaming.

So smart. He prayed to the stars that Herja would be his match.

They'd be perfect together! They were already friends... what more could they ask for?

TWENTY

Dear Kaia,

I hope that everything is going well with your family. I don't know, but it sounds exhausting to me! I love spending time with my family, but I can't keep track of all your cousins. But I guess as long as you're having a good time, that's all that matters. I think if I had a bigger family, it would be exciting to get together.

You asked me about Herja in your last letter. She's doing a lot better. She's talking with Professor Farrow again, and she's acting more like herself. She still gets mad about what happened with the Golden Forest sometimes, but she seems to be getting better about it. Penelope's good, too. She's trying to roast sausages over the fireplace and told me not to tell you she's actually burning them.

Yesterday, Headmaster Twila told us that they decided we could all invite people to come to the Institute for the Winter Feast. I asked if that meant I could invite all my family and they said yes! I'm so excited. I didn't like the idea of being away from them, but between work and travel, I didn't think I could see them. It's gonna be so much fun.

The twins are turning twelve this coming year, and I think it'll be good if they can see some of the Institute in case either of them is a witch or a dragon. Do you have any cousins going to the Silver Springs this year?

I have to go get at my chores, but I'll write again later.

Miss you and love you.

Wickham

PS: This is Penelope. They're crispy, not burnt.

⁜

DEAR PENELOPE,

I'm sure they weren't burnt. But maybe use the kitchen instead of the open fire next time. The soot might end up staining the pan. Although, once you learn how to shift into your dragon form, you won't need to have a pan at all. That'd be cool.

Wick told me that you could invite your family to the Institute for the feast. Are you going to? I wish I could come. I miss you three. But things are going well here. Madame Adora has decided she is going to go spend the break with her family. And I don't know why, but since she left, I can't keep anything tidy! We're always putting things back in their place and have told the little ones not to make messes, but I can't ever figure out who is making the messes.

Anyway, I guess that's only to be expected when we have a million people in the house. The other day, I saw a rucksack in town that reminded me of you, and so I've sent it along with this letter. I hope you like it! Let me know how the feast goes.

Miss you! Love you!

Kaia

⁜

DEAR WICK,

Wow! You've been busy. I miss you, too. The other day, I ended up in a debate with Collin about whether or not yarrow is considered a herb or just a medicinal plant, and I thought you'd know. So, is yarrow a herb?

The schloss has been crazy lately. We've had even more cousins show up. I love spending time with everyone, but it's getting a bit much. I've been working with Mama to soundproof my door. Otherwise, I don't get a moment's quiet. I've even had to lock it during the day. My favorite necklace has gone missing, and I just know that one of the little kids took it and now is too afraid to give it back or something.

We're going to have a massive Winter Feast, too. I've already decided I'm going to make five different pies. Apple, pumpkin, pecan, mincemeat, and sweet potato. I've never made sweet potato pie, and I'm a little worried that the spices are going to be too similar to pumpkin. But sweet potato and pumpkin don't taste anything alike, so I think it will be fine.

I have to admit, though, the crowds are getting to me. I keep thinking I hear noises at night, and I'm sure that it's some cousins running around upstairs or sneaking out to play in the snow. I've been having a lot of weird dreams, too, but they're kind of fun. Weird but fun. I'll write you about one of them sometime.

I hope you're doing great.

Love ya and miss ya,

Kaia

◦•❈•◦

DEAR KAIA,

Thanks for your last letter. I really appreciated seeing it. I don't know why, but I've been feeling melancholy lately. I don't understand because I have nothing to feel melancholy about. Professor Farrow and I are back on speaking terms, and we're putting together a plan for how to help me cope with my disappointment regarding the adults at the Golden Forest.

I guess maybe things just feel like they're a little stuck right now. Winter always is a bit weird. Nothing seems to move until suddenly; it's spring.

I can't really say I'm excited about Pen and Wick's families potentially coming to the Institute for the feast. But I never really cared about the feast anyway. I just don't understand why they would have their families come when they've stayed at the Institute themselves. Maybe it's because I don't have a family. Or maybe it's something else. I don't know. Most of the professors have left for their homes.

But I don't want to write too much about this. It'll pass, and this time, I'm not even going to pretend like they don't exist. I've been journaling, and that seems to help. Row thinks I might suffer from a lack of sunshine since I don't like going outside in the cold. Tomorrow, I'm going to spend half an hour on the pond. Hopefully, it will help.

Please give your parents my best. I hope you're able to find your necklace. Wick told us it got stolen.

Sincerely,

Herja

DEAR HERJA,

I'm sorry that you're not been feeling great lately. It might be because of the sunshine. My Aunt Gertrude always has difficulty in winter, too. I asked her what she does to help herself feel better, and she recommended that you just be extra gentle with yourself but make sure to find ways to get some exercise.

Also, I know you're a fan of the Vilheim Chakspear books, and I found a bunch in the local bookshop. I'd love to get you one, but I don't want to get a repeat of one you already have. Can you tell me which one you need? I tried to read some, but I just can't wrap my head around all the poetry.

I've sent a basket of banana muffins. I found a new recipe, and I think they're delicious! I tried to put a preservation spell on them, so I hope they make it. Please let me know if you like them. I hope they're still good.

Let me know about the book!

Hugs and kisses,

Kaia

PS. Have you thought about reaching out to your old friends at the orphanage? I know the Winter Feast isn't important to you, but maybe you're missing something that used to happen there. It's just a thought; please ignore me if I'm wrong. Love you and miss you!

PPS. I know you don't really like it when I say I love you. But I really do love you. You're a dear friend to me, and I want you to know that you're loved, especially when you are feeling so down.

DEAR KAIA,

Thank you. The muffins are wonderful. I don't have any of the Vilheim Chakspear books; I have only borrowed them from the library before now. Don't feel you have to buy me a present, though. I don't think I'll be able to get you anything.

It's okay that you say love you. I'm getting used to it.

Sincerely,

Herja.

PS. Love you and miss you.

PPS. That feels weird to write. But it's true.

DEAR MR. BRYCE,

I hope this letter finds you in good health. It has been some time since I last wrote to you, and I apologize for the delay. I appreciate the letters you have written to me.

It was suggested to me that I reach out and ask about some traditions for the Winter Feast. I can't really remember much if I'm honest. But also, this is me we're talking about, and I tend not to think too much about those sorts of things. I remember that there weren't any adoptions during the Winter Feast weeks. I always thought it was because nobody wanted to adopt us when they had their own families to celebrate. But that doesn't seem right, now that I think about it.

Professor Farrow told me he was writing to you for my mental health records. I would like a copy for my own personal use as well.

Can I also get my other records? I want to know why nobody ever wanted to adopt me.

Sincerely, Herja

PS I hope you have a good Winter's Feast.

DEAR MOMMA AND DA,

I guess this can be for Benton and Julie, too, but I really wanted to write this to you for the most part. I got your last letter. I'm not coming home for the Winter Feast. I know that you want me to come home, but I can't.

It's very difficult for me to write this, but whenever I think about coming home, all I can think about is the silence. Ever since I said I wanted to join the military, it seems like you stopped talking to me, at least about the important things. I know this isn't what you want to hear, but it's the truth. I felt more alone over the summer, even surrounded by the family I love, than I do when I'm alone here at the Institute.

I know you don't understand why I want to join the military. I know that you've talked about how to change my mind. But that's just the thing... I don't want to change my mind. I do want to be part of the Fire Watch. But part of being a dragon means being where we're needed most to protect Eldavon.

I want you to think about what I, and the other second-year students, have been through. You've both seen the wildness of fire. You've both fought against it, and you've seen the devastation it can cause. I might not have been on a battlefield, but I have been in battle. I know that sounds dramatic. But I have.

I have faced enemy warriors, warriors who would have killed me. They tried to kidnap my friends; they tried to take me, prisoner, too. They nearly killed people I know and care about. This is where I need to be. I need to be part of the protective wall built between our citizens and the forces that would harm them.

I wish I could make you understand, but, in the end, you can't understand the impact of what I've been through. I can't understand the impact of this choice on you, either. But I hope that we will be able to accept that, even if we can't understand, we can support each other because that's what I need from you. I need you to love me and support me.

I'm not sure what else to write. I love you. Tell Julie and Benton I love them. Give Reuel a kiss for me.

Love, Penelope.

CHAPTER
TWENTY-ONE

THE CRISP AIR tickled the insides of Kaia's nose. She inhaled deeply, letting it fill her lungs. The Winter Feast was getting closer every day, which meant the excitement at the schloss was at an all-time high.

It also meant the chaos was at an all-time high, too.

Kaia loved her family. She loved the songs and noise and games... but it was overwhelming. When she was younger, she would become utterly overstimulated without realizing it. She would have meltdowns because she needed to be away from everyone while hating to miss anything. These days, Kaia could mostly recognize the signs of being overwhelmed and take the time she needed to be alone to recharge.

Which was why, with the sun sinking in the west, she was walking the familiar path trodden down into the snow toward the millpond.

Mama had stopped her when she was heading out. "Are you all right?" she asked.

Kaia nodded. "I just need some space and quiet."

Even now, though she was far enough from the schloss that the outdoor fire was the size of a candle, she still caught the occasional burst of laughter.

Satisfied, Kaia pulled out a small folding table and stool from her pack and set it out. Then, she put out paper and a pencil.

She turned her face toward the beautiful violet-blue sky and sighed. "Write this: It's a wonderful feeling to be surrounded by people who love you. I'm at that awkward age where the adults think you have everything under control, but I think they're right. I do have it all under control."

The pencil scratched against the paper. She had tried this with pens, but they didn't seem to work. She grinned as the words she had spoken quickly appeared on the page.

"Write: I hope that your Winter Feast goes well. What sort of traditions do you have with your family?"

The pencil wobbled and fell into the snow. Kaia rolled her eyes and started searching for it, brushing the snow away. She had been struggling with how to write this letter to Nolen for some time, not entirely sure what she wanted to say.

Mostly, she wanted to say that even though she loved being with her family, she wished she could have taken him up on his offer. Maybe spending the Winter Feast at the Silent Marshes and having him escort her through it would erase her terrible memories of that place.

Before the Odentian warriors showed up, it was a peaceful place. It might be even more peaceful if she had a friend like Nolen with her.

Footsteps sounded behind her.

Kaia straightened and turned, expecting one of her cousins. Instead, her blood turned to ice. She froze to the spot, her heart slamming so hard into her ribs that she couldn't breathe. Her hand clutched the pencil as though it could defend her.

Finnegan grinned at her. His sword was drawn and pointed at her. Fury and triumph blazed in his eyes as he lifted his lip into a sneer.

"Surprised to see me?"

Kaia screamed. Before the sound could get past the sticky lump in her throat, though, Finnegan leaped forward. He swung his sword, and Kaia threw herself to one side, barely dodging it. He grabbed her by her neck and threw her into the snow.

This can't be happening!

Snow filled her coat and boots, melting against her skin. Kaia tried to scramble up, but Finnegan put his sword against her neck.

A bitter taste welled in her mouth.

No.

This can't be happening.

She was home.

She was safe.

He can't be here!

The pencil's edges dug into her palm. Finnegan lifted his sword over his head, thrusting her hand outward, pointing the pencil toward him like a wand—why had she left her wand in her room?

"Go away!" she screamed.

And he was gone.

Kaia lay in the snow, heart still hammering, her hand held out with the pencil pointed at where he had been. Her head throbbed, and she barely managed to roll onto their stomach before she vomited everywhere.

Her body ached as it had when she ran up and down the stairs in the schloss for half an hour straight. As she pulled herself to her knees, the world seemed to grow rapidly dimmer. Nothing stayed still, and when she reached for the small table, her hand missed.

She collapsed into the snow again.

A feverish heat swept through her, only to be replaced by a bitter cold. Her mind spun, and her vision went dark.

She barely had the strength to mutter, "Find me," before losing consciousness.

HERJA TAPPED her toes impatiently while waiting for her turn to check the mail. A handful of the older students had been at the desk for at least five minutes, cooing over the treats their families sent them for the Winter Feast.

Can't you go back to your dorms to look through your prizes? She brooded.

Finally, they seemed to notice her and moved off. Herja rushed to the desk, sliding her key across. Madame Julian, the human male mistress, gave her a small smile as she opened the box for the second-year students.

"You've only got one today, for you," she said, pulling out the single envelope.

"Only one for me or only one for the dorm, and it's for me?" Herja asked as she took the letter.

Madame Julian laughed. "The latter."

Herja tried to hide her disappointment. Only one? But then, she supposed it hadn't been too long since she had sent out her last batch of letters. She hurried back to the dorm and retreated to her room. There, she sat on her bed and looked to see who the letter was from.

Mr. Bryce.

Herja swallowed hard. The envelope was too thin to hold her records. Was he going to tell her he wouldn't send anything?

A knock came on her door, and Herja quickly stuffed the letter under her pillow. "Come in."

Penelope opened the door. "Did you get the mail?"

"Yes."

"Was there anything for me?"

Herja shook her head.

Penelope's face fell. She had been quite stressed these past few days, and Herja didn't like it. Penelope, much like Kaia, held a certain position in their group. Herja struggled to make up that space on her own, even when only the two of them and Wickham were around.

Wickham.

He was probably at the hospital wing again. Herja understood about working hard toward your goals, but she had to admit that she wasn't thrilled with how little time they had spent together lately. Just like in the Golden Forest, he was far more interested in his plants than anything else.

"Are you sure there was nothing for me?" Penelope asked.

Herja pulled the letter from under her pillow. "The only letter was for me. It's from Mr. Bryce. I haven't read it yet."

Penelope wandered into the room, though whether she was listening, Herja didn't know. "Have you heard from Kaia or any of the others?"

"No."

"I guess there hasn't been a lot of time...."

Herja sighed. "Pen, do you need anything?"

Penelope hesitated before she shook her head. "No. I don't need anything at all."

That was clearly a lie. Herja frowned. Penelope usually wasn't one to be so cagey about all of this. Herja patted the bed beside her. "Why don't you come sit with me? I'm nervous about reading this letter."

"If you want me to stay," Penelope said with a shrug.

Not exactly, but you seem like you want me to want you to stay. Herja repressed a huff. Usually, she would just ask directly and never mind all these attempts at mind reading. But she had been telling the truth... she was nervous about reading the letter.

Maybe having Penelope around would help.

Penelope sat on the bed, and Herja handed her the letter. "Tell me what it says. If Mr. Bryce wants nothing to do with me, just tell me bluntly. Don't sugarcoat it."

"I doubt that's what it's going to say," Penelope grumbled. She opened the letter and smoothed it out on the bed. "Dear Herja, I know you must be worried about my response, so this is to let you know that I'm sending your records as requested. They will take three or four weeks to get to you. In the meantime—"

Penelope stopped reading. "Maybe you want to read it yourself now?"

Herja took the letter. "Thanks," she murmured.

"No problem. Just..." Penelope flopped back on the bed. "I need something to do."

Herja grinned and seized her hand. "Let's go bug Wick, then."

"Why?"

Herja shrugged. "Why not?"

Penelope snorted but allowed Herja to pull her to her feet. As they headed off, Herja glanced back at her letter once. She could wait to find out what else Mr. Bryce had to say. The important thing was that her records were coming.

She just hoped there was some answer somewhere about why she was never adopted.

⁂

KAIA'S HEAD ACHED.

Every muscle in her body was sore and tired, so much so that even pulling in the air seemed like a chore. She groaned, trying to roll to her side, but found that she was locked in place.

The memory hit her. Finnegan. He'd trapped her, tied her up—

A scream burst out as she flailed, trying to free herself. Hands grasped her, and she bit at them, terror blinding her. She had to get out of here! Who knew what tortures Finnegan had planned to make her regret standing up against him? He'd cut off her fingers and toes. He would—

"Kaia." The deep, rumbling voice was familiar.

"Open your eyes," another higher but no less familiar voice begged.

Her eyes were closed. Panting, terrified of what she would find, she managed to open one. And a cry of relief burst from her when she saw not Finnegan's terrible sneer but the worried expressions of her parents. She sat up quickly and threw her arms around them.

Sobs wracked her body.

Mama and Papa held her. Slowly, Kaia understood she was in her bedroom at the schloss, not in some dark dungeon tied up and awaiting torture. It was her blankets tucked in tight around her that had made it difficult to move. Her aches were gone; physically, she felt so good that she wondered if she had made up the pain and paralysis entirely.

Eventually, Papa pulled back from her. "Are you all right, Kaia?"

"I... think so?" Kaia replied uncertainly, turning it into a question.

She cleared her throat, knowing that her vast extended family would be on the other side of the door, waiting for news. "I'm sure I am. Yes. Yes, I'm good."

Papa's worried gaze said he wasn't sure, but he kissed her forehead. "I'll go tell the others they can stop fretting, then."

"What happened?" Kaia asked quickly as Papa left the room.

Mama frowned at her. "I was going to ask you the same time. We were just starting the mallow roast when I had the premonition to find you. You were passed out in a snowbank, so pale I thought you were dead."

Kaia swallowed hard. "What... else was there?"

"What else?"

"Did you see footprints? My writing things?"

"Your writing things, yes, but no footprints. Kaia, what's going on?"

Kaia shuddered. The attack seemed like a dream now. Had a sudden fever overcome her? She pulled her blankets higher around her. If Finnegan had been there, how could he just disappear? No magic was powerful enough to send a person into oblivion.

"Kaia," Mama pressed. She swept Kaia's bangs from her forehead. "Tell me what happened."

"I don't know," Kaia whispered. The fears she stuffed down came rushing back, sending her chilled to the bone. "Mama... something's wrong with me. I think I'm going to die."

CHAPTER
TWENTY-TWO

ANOTHER DAY.

Penelope really was trying to keep herself busy. She hated having all this pent-up anxiety that only seemed to worsen every minute. Who knew that waiting for a letter would drive her this crazy?

What if her family read what she had to write and dismissed it all? What if they pretended like she hadn't written the letter at all? What if they were removing her from the Institute? They wouldn't; it would be far too extreme.

Her brain wouldn't stop worrying, though, as useless as worrying was.

She shook her head, focusing again on fixing the tear in her favorite shirt. When she had invited Herja to spar some, she hadn't expected Herja to go so fully into the sparring. She would have worn something she didn't mind getting wrecked if she had.

The door opened. Herja and Wickham strode through.

"I just need fifteen or twenty minutes to decompress first," Wickham complained.

Oh-oh. They were going to start that up again. Penelope knotted the string—it was good enough for now.

"You took an extra shift when you knew I planned a study session," Herja replied bitingly.

Penelope folded her shirt.

"I know," Wickham snapped. "You don't have to keep telling me."

Herja put her hands on her hips, frowning deeply. "And I get that you're tired, but you're the one who asked me to help you study. Why ask if you would just brush me off when I'm trying to help?"

"I'm not brushing you off. I'm saying I need a break."

"If you're going to get better, you must apply yourself and learn to push through the tiredness."

Penelope sighed. The thing about these two was that they were genuinely good friends and got along most of the time. The problem was that Wickham didn't realize how rejected Herja felt when he kept making plans for the hospital instead of with her. And Herja didn't realize that Wickham's obsession with learning the healing arts was just as intense as her drive to learn everything.

"Interruption," she declared, stepping between them.

Both her friends frowned at her, irritated. Penelope didn't let that stop her as she threw her arms open. It was a distraction, at least.

"I hereby declare this a matter of court," she said dramatically, throwing her head back. Her red hair flicked over her shoulder. "Herja, you believe Wickham isn't applying himself. Wickham, you believe you deserve a rest. Is this correct?"

"Yes," Wickham muttered.

Herja nodded reluctantly.

Penelope pointed first at Herja. "The way you just described working, pushing through the tired, is a recipe for burnout. You know what happens when a fire keeps burning without anything to refuel it?"

Herja rolled her eyes.

"Well?"

"I get it," Herja muttered.

Penelope turned to Wickham. "And as for you, you need to prioritize better. Working in the hospital wing is all well and good, but there is only so much anyone is going to teach a fifteen-year-old. You enlisted Herja's help because you want her to help you; it will not do you any good if you ignore your studies to focus on medicine."

"But I—"

"Don't but the court, young man," Penelope declared, wagging a finger in his face. "Can you honestly say you are putting in the same effort in learning as Herja is in helping you learn?"

Wickham opened his mouth, then closed it again and blushed.

"See?" Herja said, folding her arms. "Pen agrees with me."

"She agrees with me," Wickham retorted.

Penelope lifted her hands again. "I agree with both and neither of you! You both need to sit down and come up with a new study plan together, one where you won't burn out, but you'll still take the time to learn. Good?"

"Good," Herja said. "I just wish I—oh!"

Her eyes widened as she stared over Penelope's shoulder.

Penelope turned to find... Julie. Penelope held her breath, going rigid. What was Julie doing here? Had something terrible happened? And where was the baby? Where was Julie's mate?

"Jul?" Penelope finally squeaked.

Julie cleared her throat. "Headmaster Twila said it was OK for me to come up to talk to you. But I can settle in the guest quarters and come back if you want.

"I didn't know you were coming." Penelope was vaguely aware of Wickham ushering Herja out of the common room. Her hands kept clenching and unclenching. "Why are you here? Are Momma and Da okay? Benton?"

"Everyone's fine," Julie said quickly. "Just with your last letter, we decided it was better if you could have a quicker answer than the messenger pigeons. I've got letters from Momma, Da, and Benton, all with me. So..."

"Oh," Penelope mumbled. What else was she supposed to say?

"Everyone else will head out as soon as their vacation starts," Julie said, rocking back and forth on her heels. Penelope had never seen her look so awkward. "They're all coming for the Winter Feast. So."

"So," Penelope repeated. The tension was so thick she could choke. "So, you're staying in the guest chambers?"

Julie shrugged. "I can't exactly take one of your roommate's beds, can I? That would be rude."

Some of the tension eased from Penelope's body. She let out a ragged breath and gestured to the sofa. "Want to sit? How is everyone?"

Julie took a seat and rubbed her neck; it was stiff and sore from flying. "They're all good. My mate and I decided that he and the baby would spend time with his family while I'm here, and then they'll be flying out for the Winter Feast. I'm not sure I like the idea of the baby traveling, but he's a trooper."

"If you want to go back home to be with them—"

Julie clasped her hands and leaned forward. "Pen, my mate, and my baby are my priority. But they both enjoy flying, and Reuel is getting old enough for travel, especially when I'll have the rest of the family to help out with him."

"I'm not sure what you're getting at."

Julie sighed. "I know. I'm not speaking clearly about this. But what it comes down to, Pen, is that you're important, too. I will not ignore you and your needs just because something might be a little inconvenient for me."

"It doesn't sound a little inconvenient, though."

Another sigh. Julie leaned back. "You know that I'm dramatic, Penelope. Are you saying that you're going to take me seriously when I act like this?"

Penelope grinned. This was the sister she knew and loved, not the tense, angry sister who would start crying at the drop of a hat. Penelope loosened her shoulders and shook her head. "I have to take you seriously now, though. You're a mother."

"Being a mother doesn't change who I am."

Penelope laughed aloud at the disgruntled expression on Julie's face. "Maybe the headmasters will let us put a cot in the corner of my room or something. It'd be nice to have you closer around than in the guest rooms. At least until everyone else comes."

Julie laughed self-consciously. "No, I don't think so. I snore now."

"You've always snored."

"I have not!"

"Have too."

The sisters grinned at each other, then Julie got to her feet. "You know what I could go for? A soak in the hot pools. What do you say? Hopefully, it'll be a private place to talk about... more intense things?"

Penelope glanced at the door where Herja and Wickham had disappeared. She could hear their voices through the walls, which meant if things got heated, they'd be able to hear her and Julie as well. Part of her wished they could stay to have the buffer of her friends if needed, but that was the opposite of what she had been hoping for throughout the year.

Soon, they were at the indoor pools. They were magically maintained at the same temperature year-round. With their smooth rocky faces and the occasional drizzle from the ceiling, it was one of Penelope's favorite places on campus.

They went to the hot pools first. A light breeze blew in from a magical fan, and Penelope slid into the water, sighing. Her light linen bathing suit clung to her form, and with an idle thought, she realized how much her figure had changed even in the last few months.

"First," Julie said, her eyes tracing the path of one of the lily pads in the pool, "I want to apologize to you. When you told us you wanted to join the military... I shouldn't have reacted that way. It was awful of me. I should have tried to understand instead of blowing up like that."

Penelope swirled her foot through the water, absorbing Julie's apology.

"I can understand if you think I'm just talking now, but I really do mean it," Julie whispered.

"I know you do. I just don't know if I'm in the right place right now to listen." Penelope leaned her head back and gave a bitter little laugh. "I've been so angry and stressed because I don't think you listen to me, and now...."

"Well, you do have to come to terms with your sister suddenly arriving out of the blue," Julie replied dryly.

Penelope snorted. "There's that."

"If you want to wait and talk about this later, we can," Julie said, her tone serious.

"Ummm... I think it's okay, for now. I'll tell you if I get over-whelmed."

Julie nodded and let out a shuddering breath. She moved off the small bench to sit deeper in the water. It lapped at her chin. "I want to support your choice. I know, I know. I haven't done a good job so far."

Penelope bit back a sarcastic reply. She certainly never would have believed that Julie was okay with her joining the military, let alone supporting her.

"The truth is, and I know this isn't an excuse, but I'm terrified. Even just three years ago, I never would have thought you'd see battle even if you joined. Now? Now I'm starting to wonder if war is coming, whether or not you're in the military." Julie swallowed hard.

"I know. I'm terrified, too. And I think I need to be done talking right now... as you said, a lot is happening all at once." Penelope ducked her chin into the water. "I just want to be friends again."

Julie gave her a strained smile. "I want that, too. So. Let's start figuring it out, shall we?"

"JUST BECAUSE PENELOPE left doesn't mean I still don't need space," Wickham grumbled to himself. His thin shoulders hitched forward as he buried his face in the scarf. The wind was picking up terribly, but he knew that as soon as he returned to the dorm, Herja would be waiting for him... with textbooks.

"If I had known how pushy she would be, I never would have asked her to help me," he grumbled.

"Wick."

Great. Was she following him now? Wickham rolled his shoulders.

"Wick!"

That wasn't Herja's voice... he turned. Shock rippled through him when he saw his eleven-year-old twin brothers, Donnelly and Rhett, stumbling toward him.

Wickham didn't have time to wonder how they were here. Both boys were coated in frost, neither wearing a coat. Icicles clung to their eyelashes. He barely had time to dive forward and catch Donnelly as he fell. Rhett collapsed against him, sobbing.

"What happened?" Wickham cried, alarmed.

"We were... coming... for the winter feast," Donnelly said faintly.

Wickham pulled him upright, trying to wrap an arm around Rhett as well. They were both freezing!

"Attacked," Rhett cried. "Mother and Father... they're... they're..."

A chill gripped Wickham. He understood what Rhett couldn't say. His mind pushed against it. They couldn't be dead! Why would anyone attack them on their way to the Institute?

Odentia.

"Where's Tara?" Wickham asked urgently.

"She's..." Rhett pointed. "We lost her!"

Wickham struggled to know what to do. His mind was blank. He needed to get the boys to the Institute, to get them inside where it was warm. He needed to find Tara. As he looked around, though, he couldn't tell which way they had come from.

Rhett tugged his sleeve. "This way. We have to get Tara!"

Wickham hurried with them, slogging through the snow as they headed away from the Institute. How could this have happened?

CHAPTER
TWENTY-THREE

"WICKHAM!" Herja screamed, slogging through the drifting snowbanks.

He didn't seem to hear her as he pushed on ahead. His head was bent, his arms at odd angles. The wind picked up, blowing snow straight into her face. It was blinding her, making it more difficult to see where Wickham was.

The glowing portal he was heading to was far too big and bright to be hidden.

Herja's heart slammed, an echoing heartbeat in her throat as she raced, screaming again. The snow seemed to grow thicker, her feet freezing. She hadn't bothered to put on shoes before she dashed out of the Institute. The flakes were razor sharp as they bounced against her bare arms.

Her legs were leaden, and a stitch burned in her side. Every breath was like a blast of ice directly into her lungs. Was this natural, or was something trying to stop her from reaching Wickham in time?

No. Not Wick. You can't take Wick from me!

"Stop!" Herja cried.

The blowing snow dropped off for one moment. Wickham's form

grew clear—he was closer to her than she thought... but also closer to the portal.

The outlines of the two boys flickered on either side of him. Glimmers of rainbow shimmered and faded. *Chameleon Sprites.* What? Why? How?

Herja pushed the questions aside.

With all her strength, she put on a last burst of speed. Her feet were blocks of ice, but her chest burned hotter with a fierce determination. She dove, flying. She wasn't going to lose him! With a howl, she caught him around the waist.

Her momentum shoved him forward, causing him to lose balance. The two of them tumbled forward, dangerously close to the portal. Herja tried to turn herself to stop them but found herself without the strength to do so. Pain jarred up her legs, and she screwed her eyes shut, not wanting to see the damage she had already caused to herself.

She and Wickham came to a stop, both panting. Herja clung to Wickham, her fingers digging into his winter coat. He was here! She'd done it. She saved him—

"Get off," he snarled, pushing at her.

"Wick—"

"I have to find Tara!"

The Chameleon Sprites hovered overhead as though they were whispering to each other. One of them gave a plaintive cry, and Wickham howled in response. He jerked free of Herja's hold, but she climbed over him again. Her muscles trembled as she pinned him down.

"Wickham, listen to me!" she cried. "They're Sprites. Chameleon Sprites!"

Wickham blinked. His head sank back into the snow, his eyes semi-glazed. "Tara... my parents..."

Herja used her knees to pin him in place and plugged her icy fingers into his scarf, pressing them to his neck. He let out a yelp, twisting away. But his eyes watered, just as she wanted. A film of glitter pooled and dripped away. With it, the last of the spell.

"Herja?"

"Stay here," she murmured as she got to her feet.

She whirled on the Chameleon Sprites and leaped at them, trying to catch them with her hands.

They let out a buzzing noise and flitted through the portal. The light flared, then disappeared. A wave of cold washed over Herja. She stumbled on the spot, looking down to find her toes were turning blue. Not good. How long before she had permanent frostbite damage?

"Herja?"

Something warm wrapped around her. She turned to find Wickham had taken off his coat. He swayed on the spot, looking exhausted. How much did the Sprites drain from him?

"We have to get back," she said through chattering teeth.

Wickham nodded and followed her lead back through the snow. "What happened?"

"I was coming out to look for you when I saw the Sprites approach you. They were leading you to a portal."

Wickham shuddered. "I saw my brothers. They said my parents were dead. Why...?"

"Let's just get back inside where it's warm." Herja pulled Wickham back to the Institute.

They leaned on each other, both with little strength left. When Wickham saw Herja's bare feet, he insisted on wrapping them with his scarf; they were already so frozen that it did little to help. Herja wasn't sure they would make it back.

But sometime before they reached the path, powerful arms caught them both. Herja was lifted into the air, and it felt like she was flying. When she looked to make sure Wick was still with her, she found Professor Avery carrying him. She peeked up at her rescuer, Professor Sabelle.

The professors carried them both to the hospital wing. Herja wasn't aware of much. She was too busy explaining that the Chameleon Sprites had tried to kidnap Wickham.

It seemed like hours later before the two headmasters arrived to check on them. By this time, both Wickham and Herja were wrapped in blankets. Herja's feet had additionally been put into magical socks, which slowly stimulated the blood flow back into her toes and warmed her while delivering painkillers into the tissue so it wouldn't be agony.

"Headmaster Twila," Herja said, straightening. "I have been trying to tell everyone—"

"Shhh." Headmaster Twila laid a gentle hand on her shoulder. "Professors Sabelle and Avery reported already; they witnessed you preventing Wickham from entering the Sprites' portal."

"Oh."

Wickham glanced up from his bed. While he was cold, he hadn't taken the same sort of damage as Herja had. After all, he'd been dressed for the weather. "I don't understand. They told me my parents were dead."

Headmaster Valiant stiffly took a seat next to him. "Tell us exactly what happened."

A chill ran down Herja's spine as she listened to his story. Every detail seemed so vivid! It was so unlike what she knew of the Sprites not only to try to kidnap a student but especially to tell him his family had been attacked.

"What if they were telling the truth?" Wickham asked anxiously. "What if my parents...."

Headmaster Valiant shook his head. "I'm sure it isn't true; however, we will send a dragon to check on them immediately, just to be sure."

"And to the Crown," Herja said. She rubbed her sock-bound feet. They were prickling horribly, despite the painkillers. It was enough to make her eyes water, but she kept her eyes on Headmaster Twila stubbornly. "They have to know that the Sprites have turned against the Kingdom."

Headmaster Twila's brow furrowed. "We mustn't jump to conclusions, Herja. I agree it looks bad, but the Chameleon Sprites have always worked peacefully alongside the Institute. It doesn't make sense for them to act this way; there must be a reason."

"But what if Wick isn't the only witch they tried to abduct?" Herja argued. "What if they're kidnapping people from all around the Kingdom? What if this is some sort of rising and using witch's magic to—"

"Herja." Headmaster Twila cupped her face with her hand. "It's all right. We've got this. We are already sending people to tell the crown as well as check on the other second-year witches. We believe it has more to do with the events in the first semester than anything else."

Herja chewed her lip. She wanted to lean into the headmaster's grandmotherly touch, but how could she?

Both headmasters knew that the second-year students with encounter the Chameleon Sprites play-kidnapping the witches. They also knew how much the students had gone through before sending them to the Golden Forest.

How could she be confident that they weren't just telling her pretty words to assuage her fears while ignoring what was going on?

"We have this handled," Headmaster Twila repeated. "You concentrate on getting better. You did a wonderful thing today, protecting Wickham from the Sprite's deception."

It wasn't just a deception, though. They were kidnapping him.

Herja opened her mouth, but a door slammed open somewhere in the hospital wing. "Where are they?" demanded Penelope's voice.

"In the meantime, it sounds as though Penelope wants to see you," Headmaster Valiant chuckled.

Herja didn't smile back. She pulled away from Headmaster Twila and leaned back among her pillows. The two headmasters greeted Penelope as she was brought to them, then took their leave. Wickham told Penelope everything while Herja turned her face to look out the window.

The snow was falling thick and fast. And occasionally, she caught sight of rainbow glitter so quickly she wasn't sure if it was real.

***

"IT WASN'T REAL," Kaia told herself as she stood in the window.

It was the dawning of a beautiful day, and the sight of the sun gave Kaia relief from her nighttime fears. Her shoulders hitched with exhaustion; her eyes were heavy. Yet another night where she had been woken by nightmares and could not sleep.

Mama and Papa had taken her to the doctor, and nothing was wrong with her. She couldn't stop this overwhelming feeling of dread hanging over her, though. It was preventing her from sleeping at night when the quiet was just too deep.

The day was really too noisy to sleep soundly, but at least when she woke and heard the sounds of others in the Schloss, she knew she was all right.

"This has to change," she muttered, leaning her forehead against the glass.

Maybe, if she did her best not to sleep during the day, she would be tired enough to sleep throughout the night.

A yawn nearly split her jaw. Yup. That was going to be a challenge. Maybe if she napped through the morning, then had Mama wake her up before noon? She could eat lunch with everyone and then perhaps join the little ones for their afternoon stories, just take it easy for the rest of the day.

She missed spending time with her family.

A knock came on the door, making her jump. It was barely dawn. Who else was awake?

Kaia quickly moved to the door and unlocked it, opening it to find Madame Adora. "Oh! I thought you had left."

Madame Adora gave her a smile. "I came back to give you a present, knowing how you have been so stressed."

She held out a thin necklace chain, on which hung a black and white stone in the shape of a teardrop.

"It's a protective stone," Madame Adora explained. "It will keep you safe."

Kaia took the necklace. It was lovely, although heavier than she expected. As she put it on, though, she felt as though a massive weight had lifted off her. She breathed easily for the first time in what seemed like ages.

"Kaia," a couple of her cousins called, appearing on the other side of the door. "Come play with us!"

She grinned and stepped through the door. Madame Adora caught her elbow as she swayed, a sudden fit of dizziness hitting her. But it passed quickly—probably from her lack of sleep. Kaia felt far more energized than she had been in a while.

With a grin, she hurried after her cousins. Her fears were far away —it was time to play!

TWO DAYS AFTER THE SPRITES' attempt at kidnapping Wickham, Odele and Nolen showed up at the Institute. Herja and Wickham were in the common room, studying when the twin dragons entered. Penelope was in one chair by the fire, reading —Julie was off talking to Professor Sabelle about something.

Penelope hoped that this wasn't another ploy to convince her not to join the military.

"Nolen," she greeted in surprise. "Odele. What are you doing here?"

"Papa and Mami were recruited to go to the Golden Forest," Nolen said.

"Lena and Jalene have both gone missing," Odele continued. "After learning about the Sprite attack on Wickham, they figure it was the Sprites that took them."

Penelope slid a bookmark into her book and stood. "Lena and Jelene? Do you know about Adina, Icarus, and Kaia?"

It seemed impossible that three out of the six second-year witches would have been targeted. It had to be because of what happened earlier in the year, didn't it?

Nolen's shoulders slumped. "I hoped that you would have heard something. Kaia hasn't replied to my letters in a while. I thought it was just because of the winter, but...."

"If she had been taken, her family would have told someone by now," Wickham said worriedly.

"Unless she was replaced," Herja said grimly. Her hands clenched as her eyes sparked. "We have to go back to the Golden Forest. If Lena and Jalene are there, we have to find them... and we have to stop the Sprites from taking anyone else."

CHAPTER
TWENTY-FOUR

HERJA HAD JUST FINISHED PACKING her bookbag with enough supplies for the trip to the Golden Forest when Wickham and Penelope came to the common room, both looking extremely grim. Herja's heart jumped to her throat.

"The headmasters just got word... Kaia's missing," Wickham said.

Herja closed her eyes and groaned. Why were the Sprites doing this? What had made them act like this? Had the Odentian warriors somehow gotten to the Golden Forest and made the Sprites go crazy? Or was it something even more sinister than that?

"I'll go tell Nolen and Odele." Wickham headed toward Odele's dorm room. He and Nolen were sharing their room to ensure a dragon was with him at all times.

Once Wickham had left the room, Herja turned to Penelope again. "Are you going to tell me to let the adults handle it again?"

Penelope stared back at her, a crease between her eyebrows. "Herja, if we hadn't gone to the Silent Marshes last year, Professor Farrow would have been able to find the witches much faster. They would have had other adults to help them; the whole confrontation could have been avoided."

"Or not," Herja replied through gritted teeth. "Maybe they would have found the other students, but the Odentian warriors would have been even more intensive against them; maybe the Odentian warriors would have won if we weren't there."

Penelope ran a hand through her hair. "I just... don't know."

"If the adults didn't share all the necessary information we needed earlier in the year, why would they now?" Herja straightened her shoulders. "We both know that they have a different ways of looking at the world. They don't understand things the way we do; they still think the Sprites are harmless."

"Herja—"

"We need to get to the Golden Forest and get the witches back!"

Odele, Nolen, and Wickham entered the common room as Herja shouted. Her hands clenched at her sides as tears pricked her eyes. She hated feeling so emotional, but she couldn't stop herself.

Kaia was missing.

The Sprites had already come after Wickham. How long before they came after him again? The Institute itself was protected, but they had opened a portal on the grounds. How could any of them think he wasn't still in danger?

"Kaia is missing," she said, her voice breaking. "We can't just abandon her, Penelope!"

Odele joined her. "I agree. We should go to the Golden Forest. Without the adults, they will not tell us what's really going on here. It would be better if we could have Xena and Vera with us, but if it's only the four of us, so be it."

"There's five of us," Wickham said.

"You're not coming."

Herja turned on Odele, ready to spit out that she wasn't in charge, but bit it back. Because Odele was right. Wickham was being targeted. The last thing they needed was for the Sprites to get him because they brought him to the Golden Forest.

"You're not coming," she repeated, looking into Wickham's eyes. "You can't go. You have to stay here where it's safe."

Wickham's nostrils flared. He pushed his long silver braid over his shoulder as he narrowed his brown eyes. "I'm going. She's my friend, too."

Penelope laid a hand on his shoulder. "The Sprites are targeting witches, Wickham. We'll do better if you give us your healing potions and let us go. We don't have the magic we need to protect you properly."

His jaw worked furiously, but Wickham slowly nodded. His eyes never left Herja, though, and it seemed like he was trying to build up the courage to say something. She was still as she watched him, waiting... but he turned away without a word.

Disappointment hit her in the stomach, though she had no reason to be disappointed. He was agreeing with her, after all.

"I've got enough supplies in here for just over a week," Herja said, pushing that from her mind as she held up her book bag. "But since we're all going, we will need more."

Odele nodded. "It'll be best if we don't eat or drink anything in the forest; the Sprites may put magic on it."

Nolen cleared his throat. "That is fine, but you are all missing the most important part of this plan."

"And what's that?" Herja demanded.

Nolen folded his arms. "How are we even going to get there?"

⁂

PENELOPE RUBBED her exhausted eyes as she sat beside the fire, monitoring supper. It would be another delicious meal of porridge flavored with raisins. Yum.

The others were still sleeping. Once breakfast was over, she would wake everyone up, and everything would go back into Herja's bookbag; once the food was eaten, she'd be able to take a nap in the bookbag while everyone started the search again.

"Pen?"

She nearly jumped out of her skin and instantly scolded herself. What good was sitting up for the nighttime watch if Julie could sneak

160

up on her like this? She looked up at her sister as Julie joined her beside the fire.

"You look exhausted; why don't you take a nap while I finish up with breakfast?" Julie asked.

Penelope narrowed her eyes. Julie wasn't a morning person... she reached over and yanked a couple of strands of hair from her head; they remained hair rather than disintegrating into rainbow powder. Julie frowned as she rubbed her head.

"I had to be sure," Penelope said defensively.

They had been in the Golden Forest for a week now. Julie had agreed to fly them out here, and in that week, the small group had been confronted by fake Kaia, Jalene, and Lena three or four times a day. Yesterday, they tried to be a fake Herja.

"This isn't what the Golden Forest is supposed to be like," Julie said as she checked the porridge. "The Chameleon Sprites were always fun and playful. Not like this."

"I know. But it is like this. So..." Penelope gestured to her head. "Check, too."

Julie frowned at her. "I know it's you."

"You have to check."

Julie rolled her eyes, then handpicked a few loose strands from Penelope's head and yanked them out. Then she balled the red strands into a messy little ball and tossed it into the fire. "There. I knew it was you."

She held her arm out, and Penelope gratefully sagged against Julie's side, laying her head against Julie's shoulder. Her eyes were so heavy! But the birds were singing, and while there was snow on the ground, the air wasn't bitingly cold.

"If it weren't for this ball of dread in my stomach all the time, this would be a pleasant winter camping trip," she murmured.

Julie sighed softly. "I know what you mean."

Penelope closed her eyes. She'd felt closer to her sister these last few days than she had for months. "Do you want to talk about it?"

"Talk about what?"

Penelope opened her eyes again and peered up at Julie's face. "Me joining the military. And what scares you so much about it."

"Are you sure you're in the right headspace?" Julie asked. "You've been awake all night."

"Not all night. Just the last watch."

Julie stared into the fire, silent.

"If you don't want to, it's fine," Penelope told her.

"I do want to. I just don't know if now is the best time."

"I'm ready to listen."

Julie gave her a small smile, then adjusted her position, stretching her long legs out in front of herself. "We haven't had a war in many, many years. But it's still in living memory. All four of Trace's grandparents were in the military during the last war. And they were all killed. Their extended family adopted both of Trace's parents as babies."

Penelope swallowed hard. She knew there were casualties in war. Her discussions with Sergeant Baxter during the fall semester had made that clear. She just never thought that so much tragedy could befall a single family.

"Trace's mother had older siblings who remember what it was like," Julie continued. "They still have nightmares, even though it's decades later. Remembering the fear. The anxiety. I wish... I wish armies didn't exist.

"As long as other kingdoms have militaries that could turn on us, we have to defend ourselves, though," Penelope said cautiously. "Odentia has already proven they would attack if we were vulnerable."

Julie nodded once. "But I wish they didn't have an army. I wish there was no such thing as war, that no kingdoms had a military at all. I wish we could all just live in peace, knowing there would be no such attacks."

Penelope leaned forward to stir the porridge, not knowing how to respond.

"For the last few decades, we have been living in peace and comfort. Eldavon has prospered. We haven't dealt with any major natural disasters. We haven't had famines, and everyone has had their needs covered. Our arts have flourished, and everyone gets an education." Julie's expression darkened. "But it's all sitting on the edge of a blade. One invasion could wipe out all our peace."

Penelope chewed her lip, her stomach cramping.

"You wanting to join the military is a reminder of the last time there was unrest in the kingdoms. Odentia is suffering and instead of accepting peaceful help, they seem to want to steal it." Julie scrubbed her hands over her face. "What sort of world is Reuel going to grow up in?"

"Julie..."

"Trace is talking about joining the military, too."

Penelope's eyes widened. With all the silence and unspoken tension, why would nobody have told her that Julie's mate was thinking of joining the military as well? "But he's a healer."

"He wants to join as a medic. Just like his grandmother... who was killed in battle. Even though she wasn't a fighter."

Penelope's skin went cold. She huddled deeper into herself, trying to come to terms with what she was hearing right now. Her mind flashed to Wickham, and imagined him in the middle of a battle, trying to take care of wounded warriors.

It made her shudder. No, she didn't want that. She didn't want it to be a possibility.

And what if Wick ends up being my perfect match, then? Will he follow me to the military? What if it's Kaia? She couldn't imagine either of her friends being part of the military. Nor any of the witches, for that matter.

"But we don't know that it will become a war," Penelope said, trying to bolster herself as well as her sister. "Odentia's king is accepting our help now. So there's no reason for them to invade or try to steal any of our witches and dragons anymore."

"There was no reason before, either. Our aid was offered freely."

Penelope had nothing more she could say. Of course there was no reason for Odentia to do any of what they had done. And that was the reason she wanted to join the military in the first place. How was she supposed to comfort Julie when the reasons she gave for not wanting Penelope to join were the very reasons she felt she was needed?

"I have to do this," Penelope finally said.

"I know. And I'm sorry for blowing up at you the way I did. I reacted with all the emotions I had been bottling up, and it's not fair to you." Julie put an arm around her again and pulled her into a hug. "I just wish we could live in a world where..."

She trailed off, but Penelope understood.

They had entered uncertain times. Everything they thought the future would look like was now shifting and horrible possibilities were crowding in.

"I know you need to make this choice," Julie continued softly. "And I'm not going to try to change your mind anymore. I love you."

"I love you, too."

Penelope closed her eyes, letting her emotions course through her before she carefully separated them out. As much as she would like to talk more about this, they had a mission to accomplish. Kaia, Jalene, and Lena were still out there...

And she was going to find them.

CHAPTER
TWENTY-FIVE

ANOTHER LONG DAY of searching with no luck.

Herja pulled her knitted cap off and ran a hand through her hair, the frustration boiling up under her skin. Why had she thought that this was going to be a simple matter of arriving here, finding the witches, and going home?

"We should head back," Nolen said from behind.

Penelope and Julie were setting up camp, leaving Herja, Nolen, and Odele with the last bit of daylight to keep searching. That daylight had passed some time ago, the cold of the winter dark pressing in on them.

Herja turned back reluctantly.

As she did so, she caught sight of a glimmer nearby. She blinked, and it was gone. "Hey!"

Nolen and Odele turned to her, and she gestured for them to follow her as she headed toward the glimmer. Her heart grew faster as she plowed through the snow. Soon, she came to the spot where she'd spotted the glimmer.

The trees fell away, revealing a lake. The waters lapped at the frozen shore, stunningly blue even in the dark forest. Colorful lights flickered in the sky overhead, reflecting off the lake in a series of mesmerizing shades. An eerie stillness filled the forest as the frigid air bit at Herja's cheeks. Cold crept through her clothes; the silence was broken only by her own panting.

It was beautiful. The stark contrast of the dark waters and the snow-covered banks took her breath away as the trees cast long shadows over the rippling lake. It churned and bubbled, throwing out droplets that caught the overhead light like sparks.

A dark figure rose from the lake. Herja squinted, then gasped as the form of a horse became clear. Long strands of seaweed hung from it like a mane and its ears pinned back. It snorted and pawed the water. A terrible scream echoed across the lake, and the kelpie charged.

Herja fought back the urge to run. She stayed where she was, planting her feet firmly. As the kelpie drew to a stop just before her, rearing to its back legs, she leaped forward. She hurled a net over the beast's head. Nolen and Odele caught the other corners and together, the three of them brought the net down.

The kelpie vanished, as did the lake.

Instead, they were left with a single Chameleon Sprite in the net. It buzzed and trilled in anger as Herja closed the net, trapping it.

"Kelpies don't live in the Golden Forest," she told it.

The small creature twisted itself up in the net, wings attempting to flutter, but it was caught too tight. "Let me go, small two-leg!"

"I'll let you go when you tell us where our friends are," Herja snarled back.

The Sprite settled in a sad little lump. "Let me go."

"Tell me where my friends are!" Herja's heart slammed into her ribs. She wanted to scream and beg but forced herself to remain still. Her hands trembled as she kept the net shut. "Just let us bring them home."

"They're safe and happy. Why do you want to take them back to misery?"

"It's not misery. It's life. Where their friends and family are." Herja felt her lip trembling, though she fought against it. She would not cry! Not in front of the twins, not in front of this Sprite. "So just give them back."

The Sprite buzzed at her.

"Please." Her voice broke. "I don't have friends. I never let myself get close to people. But Kaia is my friend. Jalene and Lena are... sort of friends. What about my misery? What about the misery of their families and other friends? We can't lose them—we love them!"

Another buzz.

Then, the net was empty. It fell with a soft swish and Herja was left clutching at the air. She opened and closed her mouth several times, blinking rapidly. When she looked up, she saw the Sprite hovering right over her head. Nolen and Odele were tangled up in a second net.

Had this all been a magical spell?

"Stop!" Herja yelled, chasing after the Sprite, but it disappeared in a shower of colorful sparks.

"Herja," Odele called.

No. No! She couldn't have gotten so close only to be tricked so easily. Herja stood where she was, one hand still outstretched.

"Herja, we need help!" Odele shouted.

Reluctantly, she turned back to the twins. She was quiet as she helped untangle them. The three headed back to camp, all silent. Herja let Odele tell Penelope and Julie what happened as she went straight for her bedroll. She should have seen that the sprite was casting magic. She should have known somehow and caught it for real.

"Herja!" Penelope called.

She lifted her head. Everyone else was at the fire with food dished up.

"Come over here and eat. You need to keep up your strength."

"I'm not hungry."

"You still need to eat."

Herja let out a huff but came back to the fire. She accepted the bowl Penelope handed her, but only managed a few spoonfuls before she felt too sick to continue. She lowered the bowl to the ground.

"It's okay," Julie told her softly. "The Sprites are acting unusually. You can't blame yourself."

It was supposed to make her feel better—but it had the opposite effect. Tears welled in Herja's eyes. They dribbled down her cheeks before she could stop them. Her shoulders were hunched as she hid her face in her hands.

"Hey." Julie reached out to put an arm around her.

"Don't touch me."

Julie withdrew.

Herja trembled. "I swore I'd protect my friends. I promised myself I'd train harder so they would never be in danger again. And I'm failing. I can't find them and no matter how hard I try, I can't think of what I need to do. How are we supposed to find them? How am I supposed to protect my mate when I've been matched.... Who is even going to want to be mated to me?"

"Herja, you're still so young," Julie started, then fell silent.

Nolen spoke. "I'm mad at you."

Shocked, Herja looked up. Did he blame her for this, too?

He glared into the fire as he poked the coals. "You told that Sprite that Kaia is your only friend."

"I didn't say that. I said she was one of my only friends."

"But I'm not your friend." Nolen looked up and his eyes narrowed further. "I'm almost a friend, like Jalene and Lena. Isn't that right?"

Herja stared at him. "I don't understand what you're getting at."

"I thought we were friends."

"We're friendly," Herja said slowly.

"That's not the same!" Nolen got to his feet and put his hands on his hips. "You wonder who would want you as a mate? How about anyone? You're resourceful. It's not like you have to be perfect in order to be likeable, Herja!"

Herja's brows pinched together. She really didn't know what to say. Nolen never struck her as the kind of person who would stand up for her like this.

A horrible thought came to mind, and she leaped to her feet. She dodged around the fire and tackled him, yanking a few hairs from his head—but they remained here. They fell into a tangle of limbs while Odele shouted. She yanked Herja off Nolen.

"What is wrong with you?" Odele yelled.

"I thought he was a Sprite!"

168

"So, someone says you're worthy of love and you think they're a sprite?" Odele demanded. Her expression was horrified as she threw her hands into the air. "You need help, Herja! Professional help. You have a lot of trauma to unpack."

"That's not fair," Herja muttered weakly.

It was true, though.

She did have a lot of trauma.

"Hey." Penelope helped Nolen back up as she frowned at the two girls. "Yelling like that isn't helpful, Odele. And Herja? Are you—"

Something long and sticky fell over Herja's cheek just as a thin, glittering rope suddenly popped into existence around Penelope's wrist. Herja brushed at the thing on her cheek, only for her hand to stick to it.

Webbing. Her eyes widened in terror as she reached for the knife at her belt—only for her hand to be stuck on the hilt. Sprites zipped around, circling the five dragons.

"This isn't what we want!" Herja shouted.

But within seconds, she was wrapped in the sticky cocoon. Helpless.

<hr />

WICKHAM SAT in the common room of his dorm, cold despite the roaring fire. He understood this feeling too well. No number of blankets would take the chill off, not when the cold was coming from inside of him.

Just after Herja, Penelope, and the others had left for the Golden Forest, the Institute had gotten word that Adina and Icarus had gone missing. Worse, earlier today, he'd overheard the headmasters talking... Xena and Vera had both been taken, too.

Kidnapping the witches was one thing, but now it seemed the Sprites had taken the dragons, too. It made him sick to his stomach. They had heard nothing from the four second-year dragons who went to the Golden Forest. Nothing from Julie either.

It was completely possible that he was the only second-year student the Sprites had not yet managed to kidnap.

He inhaled deeply. "How many more, though? Is there something about being a second-year student that makes us more vulnerable?"

He had been trying to puzzle it out but wasn't anywhere near close to figuring it out. Why would the Sprites, who were pranksters but otherwise harmless, go around kidnapping people? It didn't make any sense! He had thought maybe Odentia had sent warriors into the Golden Forest and somehow corrupted it, but that made little sense.

He shook his head. If the adults who knew about what drove the Chameleon Sprites couldn't figure it out, he wouldn't either.

All he knew was that Professors Avery and Sabelle were at the Golden Forest right now, trying to talk with the Sprites... and that the search for the missing students now included all the dragons, not just the witches.

Wickham turned his head only to stop dead. Herja stood in the middle of the common room. She stood tall with a wide smile on her face. Her hair seemed a little longer, slicked back, and her black clothes fit her perfectly. She rolled her sleeves up to her elbow, revealing a dark bracelet on one arm and a detailed tattoo of a rose on her other arm.

Sparkles surrounded her, floating through the air like dust in sunlight.

Even if Wickham hadn't known that Herja wasn't at the Institute, the protective wards set up around the dorms specifically would have allowed him to see that this wasn't Herja at all, but a Chameleon Sprite.

Anger swept through him. It was bad enough that they had told him that his parents were dead—they weren't. They were safe at home, as were his siblings—but now they were using Herja to get to him?

"Come outside with me," the fake Herja said, holding her hands out to him. "The stars are beautiful. Let's dance and sing and—"

"I know you're a Sprite. Or a bunch of Sprites," he corrected himself. His voice came out low and harsh. "Show me your true form!"

Faux-Herja tilted her head to one side. Her form shimmered for a second before it coalesced into the same image of the woman who had greeted them at the start of the semester. "It will be easier for us to talk if I have this form. You may call me Allison."

Wickham backed up a step, putting his back against the solid wall. He didn't want to risk being caught in a surprise portal. "What are you doing here?"

"We've come for you. We have built you a new world, one where you don't have to be afraid."

"You mean you're tricking me to steal my magic!" But that didn't make sense...either... Sprites couldn't take magic from the dragons. They had no reason to kidnap the dragons, then, and yet they have.

Allison frowned. "We are not stealing anything, little two-legs."

"My name is Wickham."

"Wickham. We are not stealing magic. The others did not agree, and so we are not taking anything from them." Allison stepped forward. "Please. We have built you a happy world. You don't have to be afraid anymore. We will look after you."

Wickham's heart pounded in his ears. "What do you mean?"

Allison stepped forward again. "We can taste your fear. It hurts us. So, we created a world for you. Please...?"

And it all suddenly became clear. The Sprites weren't after their magic. They weren't corrupted by Odentia. This wasn't an attack at all.

Chameleon Sprites were empathetic. They could sense the trauma and pain the second-year students had been through in the past two years. They could feel the lingering fear that this trauma had left them.

"You want to fix us," Wickham murmured.

Allison nodded. "We can fix it. Come with us, Wickham."

She held a hand out to him. Wickham stared at her, his mind whirling. He knew why, now... nobody else did. And the others were there, in the Golden Forest.

He took her hand. "Let's go, then."

CHAPTER
TWENTY-SIX

MOTHER AND FATHER sat on either side of her as they placed the cake in front of her. Herja stared at the cake, longing to dig into it. If she concentrated, the faces next to her grew fuzzy. They looked nothing like the portraits she had been shown of who her parents were. Their voices sounded distant and echoey.

But if she stopped thinking, everything snapped into focus, which was how it always was. Her parents are here, alive. It didn't matter that she had no memories of them because it was her birthday.

"Make a wish, sweetheart," Mother said as she kissed Herja's temple.

My wish. Herja dug her fingers into the table, staring hard at the candles that flickered on the cake. What did she wish for? *To be adopted.*

But her parents were right here; why would she need to be adopted? They never died. She was never alone. She didn't have to have that pain. She didn't have to think that nobody wanted her, that she was unlovable.

"Herja, sweetie," Father said. He pushed the cake closer to her. "Blow out your candles."

Herja's shoulders slumped. She didn't want to give this up. She didn't want to leave. So she pushed those thoughts aside and focused on her cake. She knew what she would wish for—all her friends to be here.

She closed her eyes and blew out the candles.

When she opened her eyes again, Kaia, Penelope, Wickham, and the other second-year students sat across the table. They all grinned and cheered.

"Surprise!" Kaia cried. "Bet you didn't expect to see us here, did you?"

Herja laughed. "No! When did you get here?"

"We were hiding under the table," Wickham told her. He pushed a wrapped present across the table. "Happy birthday."

Herja grinned at him, her heart fluttering. She carefully unwrapped the present, making sure she didn't wreck the beautiful paper. It shimmered with shades of green and blue. To her shock, she kept unwrapping it. The paper kept getting bigger and bigger, and as she unwrapped it, it grew softer beneath her fingers.

Finally, she found a beautiful sapphire necklace when she finally got to the center. She lifted it, admiring the stone. And suddenly realized just what the wrapping paper had been.

With a delighted laugh, she set the necklace aside and lifted the dress by the shoulders. The shimmering blue-green fabric was as soft as butter as she held it up to herself. "How did you do that?"

Wickham winked at her. "Magic!"

"It's beautiful!"

"Go put it on," Kaia urged. "You're so beautiful; it will suit you perfectly."

Herja blushed but pulled the fabric into her arms and rushed into another room. She changed out of her normal dark clothes and admired herself in the mirror. Kaia was right—she looked stunning! The shades matched her black hair perfectly, and the sleeveless cut showed off her muscular arms.

Blushing still, Herja headed back into the living room. Everyone cheered when they saw her. And Wickham smiled even more widely.

Her heart slammed into her ribs as she smiled back.

Odele clapped her hands. "You really are beautiful; you know that? Beautiful and smart. You don't have to choose one or the other."

"I know that now," Herja replied.

A knock came at the door, and Mr. Bryce entered. As he came in, Herja's smile slipped. Mr. Bryce. The caretaker at the orphanage. But her parents were alive. They never died. If they were here, she never had a reason to go to the orphanage. She wouldn't have met Mr. Bryce.

"No, no," Mother said, stamping forward. "This is Uncle Bryce, Herja. Uncle."

Uncle. Right. That meant... nothing was wrong. Herja rubbed her forehead. She sat back down as Father gave her a slice of cake. After that, everyone kept pushing more and more presents on her. Books of all sorts, beautiful clothes, and even more.

Herja let herself get caught up in the celebration. She laughed at the silly stories Father told and enjoyed the exquisite sweetness of the cake.

"Let's have a dance," Kaia suggested.

Uncle Bryce played the harpsichord.

Herja frowned at it. "Where did that come from?"

Wickham caught her hand. "What does that matter? Let's dance?"

But this wasn't right. Herja pulled away from him, pressing her fingers to her temples. It felt like her mind was collecting cobwebs. She couldn't think clearly! Something was wrong. This was wrong. She wouldn't know Mr. Bryce if her parents were alive. Her parents...

"Uncle," Father insisted. "Not Mr. Bryce. Uncle Bryce."

"But I didn't say anything!" Herja cried in frustration.

Wickham reached both hands to her. "Let's dance."

"Stop it!" Herja backed away from them. The beautiful, silky dress faded from green to blue, darkening closer to black. "Stop it, all of you! This isn't right. What's happening to me? What are you doing?"

Mother stepped forward. The rest of the room seemed to fade away. She cupped Herja's face in her hands and wiped a tear off her cheek with her thumb. "You have to stop fighting us."

"Fighting?"

"You are too logical for your own good. You keep fighting it. Don't."

Herja closed her eyes, trying to clear her head. "But I don't want this."

"What do you want, then? I thought you would like the dress. Perhaps instead of a birthday, you should be at the beach? A sunny day?"

"Let me go."

Her 'Mother' let out a plaintive cry. "But this is happier. Stop fighting us. You're loved here. We want you to stay."

They wanted her. Herja lifted her head and opened her eyes. She let the pleasant fog fill her mind again. They were right... she really did think too much for her own good. She smiled and hugged Mother.

"We love you," Mother whispered. "You're perfect just the way you are."

⚜

PENELOPE STOOD ON A SMALL DAIS, her hands clasped behind her as she faced the kings and queens of Eldavon. Her back was straight, relief swelling through her chest. Odentia's king stood nearby, with the same beaming smile on his face that Momma, Da, Julie and Benton all had. Trace was next to Julie, both holding baby Reuel.

Nobody had to be afraid anymore.

King Diesel stepped forward, beaming at her. He didn't even have to use his cane as he held up a medal to slip over her head. "Penelope, you have done exemplary work this year alongside your family in the Fire Watch. Thanks to you, there have been no major outbreaks of fires throughout any kingdom on the continent."

Penelope grinned. "I could never have done it without my dear friends. Herja was the one who figured out how to apply magic to the forests to prevent wildfires, and it was Wickham who figured out how to decompose the excess foliage. And, of course, Kaia was the one who negotiated with the other kingdoms."

I'm only fifteen, Penelope thought, but it was a leaf on a stream and washed away quickly.

She had been part of the Fire Watch for years. She had to have been since she brokered peace with all the kingdoms. The military and armies in every kingdom had been disbanded. The warriors moved to help in cases of natural disaster instead.

Wait! If she was an adult, if she had spent years negotiating peace and putting an end to fires—where was her mate?

Penelope searched the crowd, her heart in her throat. At first, the faces blurred. She rubbed her eyes and looked again. The faces were clearer this time. And at the very back of the crowd was her mate. She lifted her hand, calling out to them.

But she didn't know their name.

And their face was in shadow. Veiled or a spot of blurriness, preventing her from seeing her mate.

"You have done great work," King Diesel called.

Penelope jumped and turned back to him. "But King Diesel is dead. It's King Sydney and Queen Abigail now."

King Diesel waved his hand—no, it was King Sydney. Penelope opened her mouth and closed it again. What was that?

"You must be exhausted from your long day," Queen Abigail said, patting her shoulder comfortingly. "Why don't you go to your family, my dear?"

"But—"

"Shhh." Queen Abigail shook her head. "Don't think about it too much. This is what you want, isn't it? Look at how proud your family is of you. No military. No armies. You don't have to worry about invasions because everyone gets along now."

Penelope shivered. The form around Queen Abigail shimmered, glittering rainbows smearing across Penelope's vision. "Then why can't I see my mate's face?"

Queen Abigail frowned. "You dragons are very stubborn."

"We have responsibilities. I can't stay here. What about—"

"Shh." Queen Abigail said. "You'll wake the baby."

Penelope looked down to find Reuel in her arms. His warm weight was comforting as he slept in a peaceful slumber.

This was a peaceful world for him. He could grow up without the same fear that had plagued her as a child. No more armies. No more threat of wars. Even the fires were taken care of.

Penelope gently rocked her nephew, smiling at him. This was the world she wanted for him. It was the perfect sort of world that he deserved to grow up in. Yes. Yes, this was exactly what she wanted. She headed to her family, thoughts of her mate still at the back of her mind but no longer pressing.

"We're so proud of you," Momma gushed. She hugged Penelope tightly. "You have grown into such a wonderful young woman. I'm sorry I ever doubted you."

Da kissed her head. "You are wise and strong, Penelope. Never forget that."

Penelope beamed at them, then turned to Julie.

Her sister's eyes were wide. A slight glaze filmed over the silver hues of her irises. As Julie shook her head, the glint of glitter fell around her. For half a second, Penelope could see sticky strands of webbing wrapped around her.

"Julie!" she cried.

Reuel seemed too light in her arms. When she looked down, he was fading away. Panic constricted Penelope's chest. No! No, no, no!

"It's not right," Julie whispered. "It's wrong. Pen—"

Something wrapped over Penelope's eyes. Everything disappeared, and she was left hovering in a blank, empty space. She screamed, her voice soundless in her own ears. But as she reached out, desperate to find something to cling to—

Her hand found something warm.

She stood beneath a white arch. Flowers wrapped around it, releasing their sweet smell into the air. She wore a floor-length gown, and without being able to see herself, she knew her hair was done up, and she was the most beautiful she had ever been in her life.

Across from her was her mate.

Julie and Benton stood on her side, both dressed in matching uniforms, both beaming brightly. Her parents stood nearby, leaning into each other as they wiped happy tears from their eyes. Guests flowed around them, as far as Penelope could see. Kaia, Wickham, and Herja all stood nearby, looking happy and proud.

But something was wrong.

Her vision blurred every time she turned to her mate. Penelope blinked and rubbed her eyes, but it didn't go away. She had the impression of dark curls—

"This isn't right," she murmured.

A hand touched hers. And everything went black once more.

CHAPTER
TWENTY-SEVEN

KAIA SPUN ON THE SPOT, her hands in the air as the orchestra played her favorite song. Her skirt swished out in a circle around her. She didn't know how long she had been dancing, but she did know she never wanted it to end. She laughed as her cousins danced around her. Nolen and Herja danced nearby, while Odele played checkers with Adina. Every single one of her friends was here.

And they were all safe.

The schloss's banquet hall was open to the beautiful summer weather. Birds flitted overhead and the sweet scent of flowers continued to wash over her. Kaia threw her head back as she slid herself across the dance floor.

A hand caught her wrist.

She jerked in surprise, but the sudden thudding of her heart calmed quickly as she saw it was Wickham. She grabbed his other hand and tried to dance.

"Kaia, no," he said.

Her smile faltered. "But we're dancing."

Wickham gripped her hand tighter. His expression was set and determined as he tugged her toward the exit. Outside, the beautiful summer day rapidly grew darker, and by the time they got to the doors, it was pitch black out there.

Kaia yanked her hand free and stumbled back. "No!"

"You have to come with me."

Kaia shook her head. "No! I don't want to go. I'm happy here."

Her heart raced with fear and uncertainty.

Wickham stepped toward her, then stopped. His shoulders slumped as he held both hands out to her once more. "I'm sorry. But we have to leave. We can't stay here. You can't stay here."

"Kaia?" Mama called. "Come back to the party."

"Kaia, listen to me," Wickham said urgently.

She shook her head, backing away from him.

"This isn't real. The Chameleon Sprites have put a false world in your mind. They think they're helping. But this isn't real. You have to go home."

"Kaia," Mama called, but she sounded so far away...

Wickham lowered his hand. "I will not force you to come back, Kaia. But just think about your family here. Think about how much they're going to miss you."

Kaia growled. "But they're right here! I don't have to go anywhere. Everything is fine now. Look!"

She seized his arm and pulled him back. As they headed toward the center of the dance floor, the windows brightened outside once more. Wickham stumbled, grunting. Kaia ignored this—he was just overwhelmed by the music—and lead him toward the person at the banquet table.

Wickham gasped and yanked his hand away. "Finnegan!"

Finnegan looked up from where he was helping the little ones color. Ever since he had arrived, he looked young and carefree. That horrible sneer that had been so familiar was gone forever, and the smile that broke over his face was a true beam of sunlight.

"Wick! Glad you could make it," Finnegan smiled.

"What—" Wickham looked between Kaia and Finnegan, shock clear on his face.

Kaia had to laugh. "He reconsidered, isn't it great?"

Finnegan nodded. "I decided I no longer wanted magic or any of that power that I was seeking. I was so very sorry for what I put you children through. I had to come to Kaia's family schloss to apologize. I'm so very lucky that Kaia forgave me."

"Don't you see?" Kaia turned to Wickham pleadingly. "He's working to improve himself and the loves of people in Odentia. I'm planning many social projects to help as well. Everyone is happy."

The pain in Wickham's eyes made her want to cover her face. Kaia didn't want to see that. She wanted to get back to dancing, to having fun! Why was that so wrong? Why was it wrong to be happy, to not have that terror every minute of every day?

Wickham put his hands on her shoulders. He searched her gaze so intently that she couldn't look away. He grimaced, as though in pain. Kaia's heart pounded with a renewed fear as his fingers tightened on her shoulders.

It occurred to her that amidst all the dancing and partying, his touch was the only thing that felt real.

"They're trying to take me away."

Kaia's voice trembled. "Who?"

"The Chameleon Sprites. They said I could talk to you, but they don't like it. They're trying to pull me away, to put me in a 'perfect' world of my own. But I don't want to go! It's not perfect if it's not real. My real family needs me. Kaia! You have to listen to me! You have to face reality."

"Stop."

"If even one witch agrees to leave this fake world they created, they'll let us all go. They think this is better... they think this is what we want. You must fight. Please."

Madame Adora stepped up beside them. "Kaia, we have to take your friend. He's sick. Let him come with us."

"Don't do it," Wickham begged.

Kaia pulled away from him. Her body was rigid as Madame Adora pulled Wickham away. Though his mouth moved, his gaze still locked on her, she couldn't hear what he was saying.

Finnegan stepped in front of her. "Kaia, we have to talk about crops. I think I know how to increase yield, so it will feed all the king-doms easily."

Kaia looked to him, feeling vague and unsettled. "What?"'

"The crops."

"I have to go... Wickham..."

Finnegan rested a hand on her arm. Unlike Wickham's grasp, she barely felt it. "He's sick and needs to rest. It's okay, we're going to look after him."

Kaia tried to step around Finnegan, and he stepped in her way again. Her heart started to beat faster, and she slid back, eyeing him warily.

And as she did so, she realized she wasn't happy he was there. Despite this claim of a change of heart, despite having memories of working with him for... how long had it been? It couldn't have been years, and yet it seemed like it had been years.

It was as though scales had fallen from her eyes. As she looked around, she saw clearly for the first time in what felt like forever. She had been here too long. The day outside never changed. Little ones never got bored. The food never got cold... she never got hungry, even though she didn't eat.

"Kaia?" Finnegan asked.

She felt her pockets for the wand Nolen had made her. She couldn't find it. Where had it gone? She always kept it with her these days.

"Are you alright?" Finnegan asked again.

"Stay back!" Kaia shrieked, but when she looked up to ward him off, it wasn't Finnegan any longer. Instead, Papa stood before her.

Kaia dropped her hands. Why would she be afraid of Papa?

"Are you feeling sick?" Papa asked, stepping closer. "You seem distressed."

"My wand... I can't find it."

"You don't need it, sweetheart. You're safe here." Papa held out his arms for a hug but Kaia couldn't make herself step into his embrace.

Mama stepped up beside her. "You're safe here, darling. You don't have to be afraid."

"But... it's not real."

As she spoke, she knew it was true. This wasn't real. How could it be? The real world wasn't perfect. Children cried. Enemies didn't always have a change of heart. Dances didn't last forever.

"Why does that matter?" Papa asked. "You can have a life free of pain and fear here."

Kaia pressed her fingertips to her temples. "I need to think clearly," she said, pushing magic into her voice. "I need to think."

Her mind cleared. Some part of her had known this wasn't real, but she was too afraid of what waited for her to fight. The future was terrifying. From whom her mate would be to what her adulthood would look like, all of it left her with an icy ball of fear that made Kaia feel drained.

"Stop," Mama begged.

"Why don't you want to stay?" Papa asked.

Kaia breathed out a heavy breath. "I want to live my life."

This all started when she put on the necklace, the one that was meant to protect her. But Madame Adora wouldn't have come to her room so early in the morning. She reached behind her neck and unclasped it.

"But aren't you happy here?" Mama asked pleadingly.

"It's not real."

"Why should real be so important?"

Kaia almost smiled at the petulant tone. As she removed the necklace, the image of the schloss faded around her. The only thing left were Mama and Papa standing in front of her, both looking so sad it made her heart ache.

She gestured to them. "Because my parents will miss me. My friends will miss me."

"We can bring them here."

"You can't bring everyone, though," Kaia said. "And even if you could, it's not right."

"But why?"

Kaia straightened. "Because this is a big, scary world. There are people and things out there that want to hurt us. If we don't try to change the world, it will never get better. I would be happy if I stayed here, but it wouldn't be genuine happiness. I would always be afraid somewhere deep in my heart."

Mama's lip trembled.

"I was hurt," she said slowly. "Maybe not physically, but I was hurt. And I was afraid. So very afraid. But my friends and I understand what it feels like to be afraid, now. We can help others who experience that fear and pain... and we can do our best to make sure nobody else experiences it, either."

Papa sighed. "So, you want to leave?"

"I have to. We have to face reality, for the good of everyone."

The images of her parents flared briefly, turning into a myriad of colors and sound as they became groupings of Sprites instead.

Then they, too, disappeared. Kaia was left lying on the ground. She was warm and cozy, as though she was tucked into a blanket. She lay there, breathing quietly, for several long moments before she heard movement around her. Even then, she only listened as the other witches muttered surprises.

Herja was the first to free herself from the sticky webbing that bound them. From there, she quickly freed the others. Once Kaia was free from the bindings, the cold of winter seeped in. Hunger crawled around in her belly, and she shivered, mourning that peaceful, comfortable existence she had just given up.

Wickham pulled her into a tight hug. Webbing stuck into his hair but the relief on his face spoke volumes.

"Thank you," he whispered.

The air shimmered as Kaia nodded, unable to speak. The form of a human came into existence, looking at the group with sad eyes.

"We know we made a mistake," the Sprite person said.

"Thank you, Allison," Wickham murmured.

Allison? Kaia kept the surprise off her face. The person she saw had no clear gender—but perhaps Wickham saw something different? Or perhaps the Sprites had told him before what name to use.

Besides, Allison doesn't have to be a girl's name.

"We understand our mistake and why it was a mistake," the Sprites continued. "We promise we will not make such a mistake again. The portal behind you will take you back to the Institute... we hope we have not caused irreparable distress."

"We'll let you know," Herja muttered. She grabbed Wickham's hand and tugged him away, urging him to go through first. Everyone else followed, and finally, it was only Kaia and Herja.

The Allison figure tilted their head as they gazed at her. "Do you wish to change your mind?"

"No... but I have something to ask you. About someone who is full of anger and hate."

CHAPTER
TWENTY-EIGHT

WICKHAM STRUGGLED WITH THE BELT, his hands slick with the nerves that had been building to a breaking point the last few weeks. Thank the stars, the school year was over.

After the Chameleon Sprites released all the students back to the Institute, things became... normal. Wickham struggled deeply with verbal spells, but thanks to Herja, he was now passable at it. The thing that really surprised him was that word choice mattered less than the intent behind it.

"Are you all right?" Father asked.

Wickham cleared his throat and held the ornate belt up. It must have cost his parents too much money to afford this outfit for him, but he had to admit he loved it. If only he could figure out how to knot the belt properly.

Father chuckled as he gestured Wickham over. He helped Wickham with the knot as he spoke. "I heard you and your friend talking yesterday."

"Which friend?"

"Herja."

Wickham flushed. "Er... we were just talking about her adoption records. Rather, the records from the orphanage. Because she was never adopted."

That was all he'd say about it, though. He knew Herja was struggling with what she found, and she was planning on returning to the orphanage during the summer. It wasn't his place to share any further information.

Father finished tying the belt and smiled at him. "You're a good friend to her."

"I try to be," Wickham muttered.

The only question was, how would their friendship change after the matching ceremony?

Mother waited for them with the twins and Tara, all of whom looked like they were trying not to be bored. Wickham was just glad they were here. His nerves were bad enough, but having the support of his family made him feel better.

"Ready?" Mother asked.

Wickham nodded. "I don't want to be late."

They headed to the banquet hall. Normally, the tables would be set up for everyone to eat, but tonight, the tables had all been replaced. Instead, there was a stage in the middle of the room and several long tables holding refreshments along the walls.

Wickham arrived at the same time as the others. He let his gaze move over his classmates, taking in their attire. While he had gone for a traditional set of robes, Herja was wearing a black suit, Penelope a simple summer dress, and Kaia a ballgown. The others all wore various clothes that suited them as well.

Wickham managed a small smile at the others as the twelve of them headed onto the stage. His hands were clammy, and his heart knocked hard.

The roof of the banquet hall had been removed. Whether it had been literally taken off or just turned invisible, Wickham didn't know.

"Well, this is weird," Herja muttered, stepping up next to him. "I wish there weren't so many people."

Wickham chuckled. "I'm pretty certain at least half of them are Kaia's cousins."

"Not all of them." Herja nodded toward a group of warriors. "Look, it's Victor from the first semester. What's he doing here? He's not related to anyone. I bet he'll laugh at me."

Wickham took her hand and squeezed gently. "Nobody is going to laugh at you."

Of course, King Sydney and Queen Abigail were in attendance. Usually, the kings and queens weren't involved in the ceremony, but Adina was their daughter. Wickham took a moment to wonder which dragon was going to end up with her. He was glad he was a witch; the last thing he wanted was to be matched to someone in the royal family!

The orchestra played. The advice that the two headmasters had given them the previous day came to him.

Try not to think too much. It will feel strange to dance in front of so many eyes, but the sooner you put your trust in the stars, the sooner it will be over.

Nobody moved. Each person waited for someone else to start. Eventually, Kaia huffed. She threw her hands into the air and swayed in time with the music. Wickham grinned. He stepped forward and offered his hand to her.

One by one, the others joined in. Soon, they were all laughing as they danced. Wickham lost track of whose hands he held as they twirled and cheered and danced.

When the music stopped, they were standing in two lines, witches facing dragons. Threads of silvery light twined around their hands, looping low before reaching to their fated match.

Wickham stared at the silver threads, his heart pounding shallowly in his ears. He swallowed hard and slowly lifted his gaze, following the thread... his heart nearly burst with happiness as he met Herja's eyes.

They were mates.

He knew it!

WICKHAM?

Wickham was her mate?

There had to be some mistake. How could Wickham be her mate? They were friends. She didn't understand how this could happen. She wasn't attracted to him at all. Worse, she was going to mess it up and she'd lose him as a friend!

She didn't want a romantic possibility with him. Romance was messy and complicated. She knew that and the only experience she had was writing half a novel! This wasn't fair! She was supposed to be with Icarus. They would get to know each other as mates, and fall in love without ruining anything between them.

Who did Icarus end up with?

Wickham took a step toward Herja, and she spun her head. Icarus and Vera were holding hands now. Adina and Odele stood close to each other, winding their thread into a spool between them. Jalene and Xena were next, shoving each other's shoulders. All three pairs looked insanely happy to be matched with each other. Had they known? Had they figured it out before the ceremony?

Herja's gaze moved on. Kaia and Nolen were staring into each other's eyes. Herja pulled the threads off her hands, trying to ignore the pang of jealousy. Kaia was already beautiful. But now, with her eyes sparkling, she looked even more beautiful. Even dour-faced Nolen was handsome in his dark, loose-fitting clothes.

Herja wanted to have that with her mate. She wanted it so badly, to see who her mate was and instantly know everything was going to work out.

But Wickham?

She had already proved that she couldn't be trusted to look after him. Hadn't he complained over the last four months repeatedly that she was pushing him too hard with the studying.

Not knowing what else to do, she just stood there, staring. Then she shook herself and looked past Kaia and Nolen. She knew what she'd find next; Penelope and Lena looking as satisfied as everything else.

Only...

KAIA SMILED SHYLY AT NOLEN, her heart thumping against her ribs.

She had done her best not to think too hard about who she would end up matched with. But now, as she looked into Nolen's eyes, she had this intense feeling that it was right. Everything was perfect. She would be the perfect match she could be for Nolen.

"Hey," she said, not knowing what else to say.

The crowd was murmuring. It wouldn't be long before her crazy family would come rushing up here to demand to get to know her fated mate. She was happy they were holding back for now. Right now, she wanted the world to feel like it was just about her and Nolen and nobody else.

The stars shimmered overhead, the same silver color as the threads that bound them together. She wound to her side, grateful for the excuse to step closer to him.

"Are you surprised?" Nolen asked her.

"Um... well, no, not really. I didn't know you'd be my mate, but I also spent a lot of time figuring out how I fit with all the dragons." Kaia laughed self-consciously. She flushed slightly as she brushed her silver curls behind her ear. "But I'm happy it's you."

In that fake world the Chameleon Sprites created, everything seemed perfect. But this was just another reason it wasn't.

Kaia hadn't had her mate in that world. Yes, she was afraid for the longest time of who her mate would be and what sort of responsibilities having a mate would entail. She wasn't sure if she could reciprocate any romantic feelings. She wasn't sure if she could put another person ahead of herself.

Now she knew. It was frightening, but she could do frightening things. And sometimes, facing her fears was exactly what she needed to do to grow stronger. After all, this last semester had been full of her working toward facing the greatest fear of them all...

Nolen took her hand and smoothed his thumb over her knuckles. "So... what now?"

Kaia shook her head. They had their whole lives ahead of them to get to know each other. But what *did* come next? She glanced around, trying to see whether any of them had figured it out.

Kaia soon discovered why the murmurs in the hall had increased while nobody had rushed to the stage to congratulate the matches. Because Lena and Victor were standing next to her and Nolen, bound by the silvery threads. They were gazing at each other with smiles transforming their entire faces.

But that meant...

PENELOPE STARED AT HER HANDS.

She knew they were empty. She had looked down and back up often enough.

Nothing.

Not even a hint of silver. She had no binding, no match. When she looked back up, her eyes skimmed over the crowd. It seemed like everything was a blur. Was she back in the Golden Forest? Was this some sort of trick from the Chameleon Sprites?

But then she realized that the blurriness wasn't because she was incapable of seeing. It was because of the tears building in her eyes. When Penelope wiped over them with the back of her hand, her vision cleared.

She instantly wished she didn't have to see. The expressions of the people in the crowd ranged from confusion to alarm. Even a few looks of pity as they stared at her. Even the other students were slowly becoming aware that something abnormal was happening. Her breathing quickened.

The mateless girl. That's what she was. While everyone else was worrying about who their mates were, Penelope had decided to let the stars make up their minds. Had that been a mistake? Had they thought she didn't want a mate?

Her gaze landed on her parents. Both looked shocked. No... horrified.

This wasn't right. She shouldn't just be standing here.

Shame, sorrow, and embarrassment swelled through her. Her vision blurred, thankfully once more, hiding the eyes still on her. Her cheeks flamed, and she leaped off the stage.

"Penelope!"

She didn't bother placing the voice as she raced for the doors. This was a time of celebration. The others would all want to dance and talk and celebrate. Nobody would know what to do with her, anyway. The mateless girl.

What had she done wrong?

What was wrong with her?

Sobs ripped from her even before she reached the safety of her dorm. No footsteps had followed her, so she knew she was alone. Which meant she should be able to cry... She leaned against the door, both of her hands pressed over her mouth as though she could somehow keep it from erupting.

Trembling, she lowered her hands and looked at them again.

Nothing.

She sank to the floor, sobbing.

CHAPTER
TWENTY-NINE

THE CARRIAGE ROLLED TO A STOP, bumping Herja awake. She rubbed her eyes and moved the curtain aside to see the familiar old stone face of the orphanage. Nerves jangled through her.

Her second year at the Institute was truly over. She knew who her mate was. Wickham. Even though it felt like something had gone wrong with the ceremony. Why would she be paired with Wick when Pen didn't get a mate at all? Didn't that seem backwards? Shouldn't Pen have been paired with Wickham, and Herja left without a mate?

It made little sense. Penelope claimed she didn't care, but Herja could see in her puffy red eyes that she was lying.

With a deep breath, Herja set aside her worries for Pen. There wasn't anything she could do for her, especially since she had insisted that everybody go to their own homes. *I want time alone with my family, anyway,* Penelope had said.

And Herja had her own problems to deal with.

She swallowed as she got out of the carriage. The orphanage was just as big and imposing as she remembered it, although in her mind she had erased the multitude of cheery flowers growing at the walls.

"Good to be home, huh?" the carriage driver asked.

Herja took her bag from him and paid him. She always had deliberately prevented herself from thinking of this place as home. Now she wondered if she had made her life far trickier than she had to be.

Well... according to her records, she certainly had.

She headed up the stairs, and the front door burst open. The kids that Herja knew so well came tumbling out, followed by the caregivers.

"Herja's back!" a few of the littler ones yelled, making her ears hurt.

"You were at school!" one of them shouted, pointing at her accusingly.

"Er... yes?" Herja replied, bewildered. What was wrong with that?

Two little hands grabbed her arm and attempted to pull her off balance. "Tell us everything! Tell us! Tell us!"

Herja struggled to stay upright, holding her carpet bag a little higher to make sure she didn't accidentally bang anyone with it. "Tell you what?"

"About the Institute," was the answer.

Mr. Bryce waded through the bodies, laughing. "All of you, back inside! Let the poor girl breathe!"

He beamed at Herja as he gently directed the other children back into the orphanage. Herja breathed a sigh of relief. She had already been feeling suffocated by them all! She wasn't sure this was such a good idea after all.

"We had to rearrange the bedrooms after you decided to move to the Institute," he told her. "Camilla has your old room now, but we've bunked Jasper and Edmund together so you can find your space for the summer—I know how people can overwhelm you."

Herja smiled at Mr. Bryce in thanks as he led her inside. Her book bag was slung over her shoulder, and she made a mental note to go to the library soon. The witch-librarian there would be pleased to know how her simple gift had saved all their skins multiple times.

Once in her borrowed room, Herja took off her bonnet and set it on the bed. She wasn't a fan of the bonnet, but it worked better at keeping the sun out of her eyes and allowing her to rest her head than a straw hat.

"Do you want anything?" Mr. Bryce asked from the doorway. "Or would you prefer some time to settle in?"

Herja took a moment to formulate her response. The truth was, she had a lot to discuss with Mr. Bryce. She wasn't entirely certain how she was going to fit it into one summer. As she glanced at her carpet bag, knowing her records were tucked into the bottom of them, she swallowed.

"Well... I, um, actually, I wanted to thank you for all your letters." She turned back to her caregiver and smiled at him. "I'm sorry I wasn't better at answering them."

Mr. Bryce waved a hand as though it wasn't that big of a deal. "I know you were busy. I'm sorry that I wasn't able to come to your matching ceremony. How was it?"

"Oh—" Herja opened her bag and put her stuff away just to give her hands something to do. "It was fine, I guess."

"That sounds like something's wrong... do you want to talk about it?"

Herja chewed her lip. Out of everyone she knew, Mr. Bryce wouldn't have the faintest idea of what a fated mate actually meant. He was human; he chose his wife. But then, maybe that would mean he'd be even better at giving her advice? He didn't have a pre-convinced notion of what it was supposed to be?

"I was matched with my best friend," she finally said.

"Isn't that a good thing?"

Herja shrugged. "It should be. I just don't know how to think about it, I guess. But that's all I want to say on the matter." She pulled out her records and held them out to Mr. Bryce. "I want to talk about this. About why I've never been adopted."

<hr />

WICKHAM PRESSED his arm over his mouth to hide the yawn. He didn't want his father to think that he was too tired for this... he had been looking forward to fishing in the early morning for ages! It was the best time to think, when the sun was just waking up and the world grew restless.

His efforts were in vain.

"That's a monster," Father said, chuckling. "You sure you wouldn't rather go back to bed?"

"Positive," Wickham said firmly. He settled down on the edge of the riverbank and sorted out his fishing gear. "I want to get as much fishing in before I start working with Kassandra at the herbalist shop again next week."

Father nodded as he reached over to help Wickham untangle his lines. "I wish you would give yourself some more downtime before you start working again... maybe you can ask Kassandra to keep you part-time for the first week?"

Wickham shook his head. While he enjoyed having downtime, who didn't—*Herja*—he wanted to build up his savings right away. "I've got a bunch of different ideas that I want to try. I'm planning on making a trip to the Silent Marshes just before the next school year begins, 'cause then I can collect a few more rare plants. That's going to cost money."

"What about visiting your match?"

Wickham flinched.

Father clucked his tongue in the way he always did when he knew more than what Wickham was telling him. He must have noticed the icy way Herja had said goodbye, the distracted look on her face.

I shouldn't be so caught up in such micro details. Penelope has it much worse.

Wickham flinched again. Penelope wouldn't talk to any of them about the matching ceremony... he wasn't sure what was going to happen.

"You want to talk or let it lie?" Father asked. After a moment of silence, he continued. "It's okay if you don't want to talk. Just know that I'm here to listen whenever you do."

"I like her," Wickham blurted. His cheeks flamed as he finally looked up. "I like her more than she likes me. I was thrilled when I saw she was my fated mate... but I think she's disappointed. I shouldn't say I like her more than she likes me. I like her in a romantic sense. She likes me as a friend."

"I see," Father murmured.

Wickham nodded miserably. Just because they were matched, it didn't mean that they were romantically matched. It would have been better for Herja if she had matched with someone who could see her only as a friend... there was a lot of pressure between them, now, he thought.

"I just don't know what is supposed to happen now," Wickham admitted, feeling low and sorry for himself. "I thought that it would make everything clear, but she didn't even want to hug me goodbye. She hates that we're matched; I just know it."

"You don't know that."

"I do. It was clear enough on her face the night of the ceremony."

Father shook his head, that slow shake that said Wickham needed to get out of his pool of self-pity. Wickham didn't think he was in a pool of self-pity at all.

"Wickham, you can't read minds. Has it occurred to you that she noticed what happened with your friend Penelope and was worried about her, rather than reacting to you being her match?"

Oh. No. It hadn't occurred to him at all. Wickham chewed his lip, trying to remember the details of her expression. But even though it had only been a few weeks ago, he wasn't sure what was real and what he was making up, now that Father had introduced another possibility.

"I'm not saying that Herja has a secret crush on you," Father added in a gentle tone. "It's rough to have unreciprocated feelings, but the worst mistake you can make is to read into everything she does as either flirting or rejection. Feelings change—and that includes yours."

Wickham sighed unhappily.

"My advice to you is to concentrate on being her friend. Don't wait for her to fall in love just because you're matched. It's not fair to you, and it's cruel to her." Father patted his back. "I know you're a good kid, Wick. You'll figure this out. You've been her friend for two years now. All you have to do is just keep that up."

Wickham nodded. He was disappointed that his father hadn't encouraged him to share his romantic feelings or tell him that Herja might change her mind.

But Father was right. Being her friend for the sole purpose of hoping Herja changed her mind would be cruel to her. He straightened up his supplies as he mulled the words over in his head. He could be a friend. A good friend, the sort that didn't try to force a romance.

Fated mates weren't always romantic. It was just one of those situations. He might have been hoping it would be a romance, but oh well. Herja was too important to him for Wickham to ruin their relationship, pining after something that wasn't going to happen.

"Fifteen is too young for romance, anyway," Wickham declared aloud. "I saw how the possible romances made everyone's heads go screwy this year. We have to concentrate on learning, not love. That's that. I'm not even going to date until I'm at least twenty-five." He grinned up at Father. "Just like you."

Father laughed. "It's all right if you want to date before you're twenty-five."

"I don't."

"All right, then." Father ruffled his hair and sat back, flicking his rod out into the river. "Let's get some fish."

Wickham settled down and started to cast his own line. But despite the radiant smile on his face, he was still unsettled inside. But there wasn't anything he could do about that, right? He just had to take it one day at a time... his feelings would change.

And he would make sure they did because he would not lose Herja as a friend.

CHAPTER
THIRTY

PENELOPE PULLED her blankets over her head quickly, just as the tent door opened. Her family had spent the morning at the latest Fire Watch meeting, and she had taken the time to get some food, wash up, and change her clothes.

But the thing about all of this was she didn't want to talk to them.

She felt terribly guilty for shutting them out when she had spent so long wanting them to open up for her. But she wasn't ready to talk about what happened at the matching ceremony. She knew they wanted to talk to her about it. But no matter what they said, it only made things worse.

So, it was better to just pretend like she was asleep, for now, at least. She'd watch Reuel later on. Spending time with the baby always made her feel better.

"Sleeping on the couch again," Benton murmured. "I'm worried. Are you sure there isn't anything the headmasters can do?"

"We talked to them; they said while rare, it wasn't unheard of," Momma replied.

Da hummed his agreement. "There's a chance that she just hasn't met her match yet. Or perhaps the stars have chosen a different path for her. We just have to give her time... it's a tremendous blow to be left without a fated mate."

"I can't imagine," Benton murmured. "If I didn't have—"

This was even worse than them trying to make her talk about her feelings. Penelope threw her blankets off and jumped to her feet. She glared at them—and the guilt only punched her harder at the startled looks her parents and brother gave her.

"Stop talking behind my back!" she seethed.

It was her own fault. She knew that. But it didn't make her feel any better. If anything, it only made her feel worse. All she wanted to do was to scream and cry all the time, and she hated feeling this way! Her hands clenched and unclenched, but she had no words.

Penelope headed for the door.

"Pen," Benton started, moving to step in front of her.

"Benton," Momma admonished. She put her hand on Benton's arm and pulled him aside. "We're having lunch in half an hour."

"I already ate," Penelope replied, taking another step to the door.

Momma's eyes were so sad that it made Penelope flinch. She fidgeted on the spot as she struggled to know what to say. But no words came, only a lump in her throat.

She hurried past them into the bright morning sunshine.

As she walked, she felt herself sinking into that pool of misery that she had dwelt in far too often these days. She knew she had to do something to get herself out of it, and soon. But she wasn't sure what to do.

It wasn't easy fighting her own thoughts.

Bad enough that her life's plans went out the window when she decided to join the military, but now everyone pitied her. Even the humans of the Fire Watch, those who didn't have mates, looked at her with those 'poor girl' eyes. But how many were wondering what she had done to deserve this?

"It's not fair," she muttered to herself.

"No, but life rarely is."

Penelope jumped. She hadn't even noticed Julie had joined her. She scowled, although thankfully Julie hadn't brought Reuel with her. "I want to be alone."

"Tough." Julie folded her arms. "As you so eloquently pointed out, being silent doesn't fix the issue. Scream at me if you must, but you are going to share what you're feeling."

"You can't make me."

"No... but I can bribe you."

Penelope's frown fell away. "What?"

Julie grinned. "Talk to me about it, and I'll get Momma and Da to agree to let me take you shopping. My treat, all expenses paid."

Oh. That did sound good. Normally, Penelope wasn't super invested in shopping. But right now, anything to get her away from the camp was appealing. And away from the eyes that knew something was bothering her.

"I guess," Penelope reluctantly agreed.

They kept walking, with Julie quiet now.

"Something must be wrong with me. Maybe I wasn't supposed to be a dragon. Maybe I stole it from Victor."

Julie gave her a startled look. "No. Mistakes don't happen at the Silver Springs."

"But what if—"

"No," Julie repeated firmly.

Penelope huffed. "I thought you wanted me to share my thoughts."

"I do. But I can also tell you when those thoughts are wrong." Julie took Penelope by the shoulders. "The only reason you didn't get a mate at the ceremony was because your mate wasn't there. If Victor wasn't there, Lena wouldn't have had a mate either."

"Do you... really think so?"

Julie nodded. "Remember how in the Chameleon Sprites' fake world, you couldn't see your mate's face?"

Penelope nodded.

"Maybe because you didn't know them yet. Kaia had Nolen as her mate in her visions. The same with the others; they all saw who they ended up with." Julie put an arm around Penelope's shoulders. "Be patient, Pen. It will all become clear. I promise."

"You can't really promise that, though."

Julie nodded. "Maybe not. But I can believe."

Believe. Penelope made herself smile, feeling lighter, somehow. She couldn't believe Julie, no... but she could hope. And for right now, hope was all she needed. The future would take care of itself. She just needed to give herself time.

━━━━━

"KAIA?"

Kaia turned to see Adina approaching. The normal beaming smile on the other witch's face was replaced by a nervous scowl. Kaia's heart started going faster; she had a feeling that she knew what that meant.

The sooner this was over, the sooner she and Nolen would be able to return to the schloss. They had talked in depth and had decided to split the summer between their families. First, they'd be staying with Kaia's family, but then they'd finish up the summer at the Silent Marshes. She was keen to get started in the summer.

Now, though, she had business to take care of. She straightened as she turned to Adina. "The delegation from Odentia has arrived, haven't they?"

Adina's eyes widened briefly, but she schooled her expression quickly. "Yes. My parents asked me to come and get you. But if you don't want to, you don't have to."

Kaia gave her a small smile. "I do want to. I asked them specifically that I be allowed to attend."

She headed toward the diplomatic wing, but Adina caught her wrist, searching her gaze.

"Kaia, Finnegan is with them. I have no idea why he was allowed back into Eldavon; I do not know why they released him from jail in the first place—"

"I've been working with your parents for this."

Adina released her hand. Her eyes widened, and she stared with abject horror at Kaia. "Why?"

202

It was a question she had been asking herself fairly often these last few months. "I'm still terrified of him, don't get me wrong. But I want to look him in the eye again. I want to see what he's really like when he doesn't have the power of our lives in his hands."

"But why bring him here?" Adina demanded.

"How else was I going to see him safely?"

Adina twisted her hands. Then determination crossed her face, and she rolled her shoulders back. "Odele says I'm braver than I think."

Kaia held out a hand. "Let's face him together, then."

As they headed to the diplomatic wing, Kaia's mind turned to that fake Finnegan from the Chameleon Sprite's world. She knew he wasn't going to be like that, but she also somehow felt like he would not be the terror that he had been in the Silent Marshes, either.

Kaia and Adina hesitated outside the doors before they knocked; they were escorted in by armed guards.

The Odentian delegation was standing before King Sydney and Queen Abigail. They all bent respectfully toward them. Kaia focused on Finnegan right away. He was the only one in chains, and the only one forced to be on his knees. Even though she was grateful he was restrained, her heart still shuddered to see any person treated in such a way.

"Adina, Kaia," Queen Abigail greeted. She held her arms out, and Adina quickly moved into her mother's embrace.

Finnegan lifted his head. That sneer that haunted Kaia's dreams was on his face, but as she met his eye... the terror faded. He was young. Professor Farrow had said he was young, but it was only now that Kaia saw how young. He could only be six or seven years older than she was. Barely into adulthood.

"Do you want me to say I regret my actions?" Finnegan snarled at her. "Is that why you've had me dragged from my dungeon to be forced to my knees before you?"

Fear glimmered in his eyes. Shock rippled through Kaia and with it, an unexpected pity. What sort of life had driven him here? And was it too late for him to choose a new path?

"I wanted to look you in the eye," Kaia told him, and to her surprise, her voice was calm. "I wanted to know if my nightmares were worth it. I wanted to see if you really were evil incarnate and if I would spend the rest of my life in terror of you."

Finnegan blinked rapidly. His expression faltered, then hardened. "I see. You mean to have me murdered, then!"

Kaia shook her head. "I want to give you a choice. You said that you're locked in a dungeon... there are creatures in our Kingdom that may be able to free you from that prison. You will be trapped in your own mind, but they will give you pleasant dreams. They'll make sure that the world you experience is one of happiness, and they will care for your physical body in the meantime."

King Sydney cleared his throat. "We have made negotiations with your brother. He has agreed to turn you over to us to serve the rest of your prison sentence. The choice is to either live in one of our prison complexes or take Kaia up on her offer and go to the Golden Forest."

"I don't—" Finnegan closed his eyes. "Do whatever you wish. I care not."

"I wish you would," Kaia murmured. "I think you could learn a great deal from the Chameleon Sprites."

But he didn't open his eyes again, refusing to speak. Kaia gazed at him, finding herself pitying him more with every passing moment. She turned, no longer needing to face him.

She bowed toward the king and queen and took her leave, the weight of a year's worth of fear lifting off her.

She might not know what the future holds. It might be painful and frightening. But she would face it all because there was no point in hiding. Not when there were people out there she could help.

The End

If you enjoyed this book, please consider leaving a review on Goodreads, Bookbub, or your favorite retailer. Reviews help me reach new readers.

Read *The Quest for the Phantom Feather*, the third book in the *Defenders of the Realm* series!

OR

Read *A Summer of Courage*, the third Fantasy Romance Novella in the
Defenders of the Realm series!

OR

Have you read the prequel?
A Journey to Power

Join my Newsletter for writing updates, sales and giveaways!
www.mhlebeault.com

www.ingramcontent.com/pod-product-compliance
Lightning Source LLC
Chambersburg PA
CBHW032002240626
47153CB00003B/1093